MY PERFECT VALENTINE

As Carissa and Rafe neared her house, it began to snow. Impulsively, she stuck out her tongue and caught a flake on its tip. There were few things that made her forget how self-conscious she usually was, but freshly falling snow was one of them. "I just love snow!" she exclaimed. She turned her face to the sky and closed her eyes.

"I can see that," he chuckled, brushing the snow from her long blond hair. "Carissa," he said suddenly. "You realize, don't you, that I still don't know anything about you? We spent the entire afternoon talking about *my* favorite foods and books and movies."

"I'm sorry, I was just . . ."

"Don't apologize. Just do something about it." His brown eyes were dancing with mischief.

"But what can I do? I guess I could—"

"Go out with me on Friday night? Give me a chance to ask *you* some questions. Deal?"

"Deal."

"Great! G'night, Carissa. See you at seven on Friday."

He asked me out! huge gulping breath o the me out!

BANTAM SWEET DREAMS ROMANCES

My Perfect Valentine

Judy Baer

BANTAM BOOKS
TORONTO • NEW YORK • LONDON • SYDNEY • AUCKLAND

RL 6, IL age 11 and up

MY PERFECT VALENTINE
A Bantam Book / October 1990

ISBN 0-553-27649-2

Published simultaneously in the United States and Canada

*Bantam Books are published by Bantam Books, a division of Bantam
Doubleday Dell Publishing Group Inc. Its trademark, consisting of
the words "Bantam Books" and the portrayal of a rooster, is
Registered in U.S. Patent and Trademark Office and in other
countries. Marca Registrada, Bantam Books, Inc., 666 Fifth Avenue,
New York, New York 10103.*

*Printed and bound in Great Britain by
BPCC Hazell Books
Aylesbury, Bucks, England
Member of BPCC Ltd.*

Happy Birthday to Connie, Janet, Kathie, Ruth, and Brenda. May we celebrate for many years to come.

Chapter One

"He's a jerk, Carissa. Be glad you're rid of him." Julie Owens's expressive features crumpled into a mask of distaste. "A first-class jerk." She brightened suddenly. "Think of it as losing weight. How many girls could go on a diet and lose a hundred and seventy pounds"—she paused to snap her fingers—"just like that?"

"You didn't think he was a jerk yesterday," Carissa Stevens reminded her friend. She could feel another round of tears threatening and reached for a tissue.

Her fingers touched the bottom of the box. Empty. It figures, she thought. Everything in her life was coming up empty these days.

"Yesterday I didn't know what he was going to do," Julie retorted. "The big . . . jerk."

"Good vocabulary, Jules." Carissa gave her best friend a lopsided grin. "Can't you think of another word besides jerk?"

"Not one that fits—or that my parents would approve of! Here, use these." Julie leaned across the twin bed on which she was perched and handed Carissa a fresh tissue box. "But you've got to quit crying soon. I couldn't find any more of these in the bathroom."

Carissa wadded up a handful of tissues and dabbed at her eyes. "What a way to start the new year. If things go downhill from here, I'll be flunking out of school by spring break."

"Very doubtful. I can't believe he was fooling around with Miss Look-At-Me-I'm-A-Pom-Pom-Girl during Christmas vacation while you were away with your family in Vermont. I just can't believe he did it!" Julie flung herself across the bed. "How could he break up with someone like you for a . . . midget!"

"Being petite is a lot different than being—"

"Tall and statuesque, like a model! Not short and stubby. I'll bet Tina Walters doesn't even come up to his elbow."

"Right. She's delicate; I'm a moose," Carissa groaned. "There's no way around it."

"Five foot ten is hardly mooselike." Julie rolled over onto her back. "Anyway, you're beautiful. Tina's nose is so short it looks like an afterthought."

"Good try, Jules, but you and I both know that Tina Walters is one of the cutest girls at Ridgewood High." Carissa sighed. It was an odd position to be in, defending her successor. She wanted to be furious with Glen, but she kept getting angry at herself instead.

"Have you looked in a mirror lately? I'd give my stereo system for hair like yours—thick, blond, and shiny!"

"Shiny? Like my nose?" Carissa quipped.

Julie ignored her. "And your smile! No braces—never had 'em, never will! Besides that, you carry a four-point grade average. You've got beauty *and* brains. Give yourself a chance, Carissa."

"Thanks, Julie. It's just awfully hard to believe any compliments after . . ." She felt another sob coming. ". . . you know. . . ."

She and Glen Matlock had been going steady for sixteen months, since the beginning of sophomore year. And now, suddenly, without warning, he'd called it off. He wanted to "play the field," he said. The field, it seemed, consisted of only one person: Tina Walters.

Carissa swung her legs off the bed and walked to the window, completely unaware of how true Julie's words were. She *was* model-like—she moved with an easy grace, and her long blond hair swayed at her shoulders. Her blue-green eyes, even puffy from tears, were beautiful—large and expressive.

"I know why he did it, you know," Carissa said.

"Why Glen wanted to break up? Because he had a lobotomy and didn't know any better?"

"No," Carissa said without cracking a smile. "Because I'm no fun."

That statement left even Julie speechless. "What do you mean by that?"

"You know me, Jules. I'm so shy it hurts. I never dreamed I'd ever have a boyfriend—especially not one as great as Glen Matlock."

"You're only quiet until you get to know people, Carissa."

Carissa shook her head emphatically. "That's not true, and you know it. I freeze up in a crowd. I feel like I'm ten feet tall and everyone is staring at me. My mouth and my brain quit working, and I act like an idiot."

"Get real, Carissa. You're too hard on yourself."

"You're denying that I'm shy?"

4

"No, but—"

"That I fade out in a crowd?"

"Not exactly—"

"That by the end of an evening, if you or Glen aren't around to help, I'm not sitting in a corner like a potted plant?"

"You've never acted like a potted plant!"

Carissa had to laugh then. "All right. But you get my point. Tina Walters is vivacious and exciting. Why *shouldn't* Glen want her instead of me?"

Julie sighed and raked her fingers through her tousled brown curls. "Okay. So you're shy. That's no reason for him to dump you."

"Isn't it?" Carissa stared long and hard at her friend.

"Well, maybe you did depend on him too much," Julie admitted. "Just a little too much. Maybe he did get tired of that."

"He said that I needed to get out and meet other people."

"Like he met Tina?" Julie's tone was scathing.

"Maybe I smothered him, Jules. It was just so wonderful to have a handsome, attentive guy who didn't mind how shy I was."

"You were good for his ego, if you ask me."

"Maybe, for a while. But even egos need a

change of pace. It's my fault that he wanted to leave. I drove him away."

Julie scooted to the foot of the bed. Her lower lip jutted forward and her brow furrowed —a sure sign that she was hatching a plan. When she looked up, she had an intense look in her eyes.

"Then just forget him! Forget Glen Matlock ever existed!" She waved her arms in the air. "Whoosh! Vanished! Ancient history!" Her expression turned impish. "After all, there are lots of fish in the sea, birds in the air, and boys in the classroom."

"Forget him? Just like that?" Carissa shook her head. "Isn't that a pretty big request?"

"You've been hung up on one guy for over a year—but there are lots of delicious guys out there. Look at me! Am I starved for male companionship?"

It was all Carissa could do to keep from laughing out loud. Julie was as flamboyant and interesting as a human being could be. From her makeup (one blue contact lens and one green on occasion, just to see who'd notice) to her clothes (Salvation Army specials, her mother's cast-off Dior dresses, or preppy sweaters) to her nonstop chatter, Julie was one of a kind. And it was a kind boys liked.

"Jules, you'll never starve for companionship. But I'm hungry already."

It was hard for someone like Julie to understand, Carissa thought. Even their own friendship had started out for Julie as some sort of humanitarian project—like being kind to a stray—when they were freshmen. Then something had clicked between them, and they'd grown to be great friends. But Julie could have fun flirting with a lamppost, Carissa mused, while she'd never learned the art at all.

Then Glen came along. He was popular, outgoing, handsome, and—an added bonus— over six feet tall. Between him and Julie, they'd filled in all the gaps that shyness made in Carissa's personality. Suddenly she'd found herself in the exciting world of the popular crowd. It always seemed like a dream, Glen Matlock wanting her at his side. And now, after sixteen months, the dream was shattered.

"You need a plan, and I know what it is." Julie paced Carissa's small bedroom. "We're going to show Glen Matlock a thing or two. That is, *you're* going to show him!"

"Show him what?" Carissa asked wearily. Between her crying and Julie's nonstop energy she was feeling tired.

"Show him that you don't care."

"But I *do* care."

"I know that, and you know that, but we don't want *Glen* to know that! Act like it doesn't bother you. Make him think you're glad!"

"Glad? How could I be—"

Julie put a finger to Carissa's lips. "Don't talk like that. Haven't you ever noticed that if you're feeling down but pretend you're happy, pretty soon you *are* a little bit happy?"

"I guess so, but . . ."

"Same principle applies here. Act glad that Glen dumped you and—"

"And I'll *be* glad? Come on, Julie. That's farfetched even for you."

Julie dropped back onto the bed and stared at her friend. "What is it you want, Carissa? Really, down deep?"

Carissa sighed. "I'm not sure anymore. To have Glen back, I suppose."

"Even after he dumped you?"

"Maybe not, but . . ." How could she explain to Julie that she'd viewed Glen as her only hope? What other boy would want a shy bean pole like her?

"Personally, I think you're crazy to want the two-timing jerk. Think of all the great boys you haven't met yet!" Julie licked her lips theatrically. "It's a smorgasbord out there! Go for it!"

"And how do I do that?"

"Hold up your head, dry your eyes, put on your sharpest outfit, and tell the world 'Here I come!' "

Carissa grimaced. "Who'd believe me?"

"Maybe they wouldn't believe the *old* Carissa Stevens, but they'll believe the *new* one. B.G. versus A.G."

"Huh?"

"Before Glen versus After Glen. You're a new woman." Julie grew somber. "You don't want people feeling sorry for you, do you?"

"No. That's even more humiliating."

"Then make 'em think you're happy! Act like you don't have a care in the world." Julie slapped her thighs. "And your first opportunity is coming up soon."

"What opportunity?" Carissa asked warily. Listening to Julie's pep talks in the privacy of her bedroom was one thing. Acting out her plan in public was quite another.

"The first committee meeting for the Valentine Ball is today. Had you forgotten?"

The Valentine Ball! She could hardly forget Ridgewood High's major social event of the winter. It was especially important this year because the Grass Roots had agreed to play.

The Grass Roots were a group of former Ridgewood students who had made it to the big time. They'd cut two records and played gigs as backup band to big-name stars. Since they were already booked in the region, they'd agreed to play for the Valentine Ball.

"Oh, Jules—I can't go to that committee meeting. Glen will be there!"

"But you agreed to be on the steering committee! Everyone is counting on you. You've got the most organized head in the school. We need you."

"But Glen was the only reason I joined the committee. He thought it would be good for me to get out with other people. And we'd be working together. Now we won't even be going to the ball together. I can't go. I *won't* go."

"You can't let Glen stop you! The Valentine Ball is *the* big event. It's an honor to be on the planning committee, Carissa. You can't back out now."

"Watch me." Carissa began pulling her sweatshirt over her head. "I'm going to take a shower. You go to the meeting."

"No way. Not without you." Julie grabbed her friend by the arm. "Where's that emerald green sweater we bought at the mall last week?"

"In my drawer, where it's going to stay."

Julie rummaged through the chest until she came up with the bright new sweater. She held it up to Carissa's chin.

"Perfect. It does incredible things for your eyes."

"I don't want things done to my eyes," Carissa said grumpily. "I want to take a shower."

"After the meeting."

Carissa glared at Julie. "Don't you understand at all? I *can't* go to that meeting and sit across the table from Glen and act like nothing happened. I was supposed to be his date. Now he'll be going with Tina, and I'll be sitting at home. There's no way I'll help plan that. What if I ended up on some committee that required me to be at the dance? It would be just too humiliating."

"Is that any worse than the way you'd feel hiding out at home? Pretending you're having fun doing your toenails and playing word games with your parents? Come on, Carissa. This is the best way."

Carissa dropped her forehead into her

11

hands, and her long blond hair tumbled over her face. "I can't, Jules. I just can't."

Julie stared helplessly at her friend's bowed head. After a long silence, she spoke.

"All right. Have it your way. Pass up a golden opportunity to meet new guys. Spend the rest of junior year mourning the loss of a jerk. Waste the best years of your life. Go ahead. See if I care." She paced dramatically around the room. "Don't follow my advice! Don't find another date for the Valentine Ball. Forget that Ridgewood is a big school, and there are tons of boys roaming the halls! Spend your time mooning over a fickle guy who dumped you because you're a little too shy and quiet! Act even more shy and quiet—that should *really* fix everything!"

Julie gathered her jacket and books from the corner where she'd dumped them. She jerked on her wool scarf with a vengeance, nearly strangling herself, muttering all the while.

"All Glen wants is a girl to take to the dance. He doesn't care if she's nice or sweet or kind or smart. He just wants a trophy to hang on his arm. . . ."

Carissa straightened her shoulders and stared at her friend. Julie was still muttering and slamming her books around in typical Jules fashion. Carissa lifted a hand to her mouth to hide her smile.

Maybe, just maybe, if she did as Julie said—acted as though it didn't matter that she and Glen were no longer a couple—it might be the best thing for her. Maybe if she were more like the perky, redheaded Tina, he wouldn't have left her in the first place.

The first genuine smile Carissa had felt in hours crossed her face. She would show Glen what he was missing. If he saw her with other boys, having fun, being outgoing, he'd realize he'd made a mistake. Anyway, it was worth a try.

Carissa astounded Julie with her next words.

"Let's go, Jules! We're going to be late for that meeting!"

Chapter Two

"Huh?" Julie froze to the spot, her left hand holding her hat over her head, her right hand reaching for her backpack.

"I said, we'd better get going or we'll be late for our first meeting."

"Run this by me again?" Julie murmured, looking confused.

"I said that we're going to the meeting after all. I changed my mind."

"But why?"

Carissa pulled her green sweater over her head and adjusted the collar of her blouse beneath it.

"Because you're the most people-smart person I know. And you're right about not sitting at home suffering."

"And?" Julie urged her.

"And because I decided that Glen Matlock shouldn't ruin my life."

"That's it!" Julie grinned widely. "Good girl." She linked arms with Carissa and did a little jig. "Look out, Glen Matlock! Here she comes!"

Carissa didn't feel so brave, however, as they approached the home economics classroom where the committee meeting was being held.

"I think I made a mistake, Jules. If I just go home now, before anyone has seen me . . ."

"And not show off that great makeup job? No way, I worked too hard on it. You look gorgeous. That sweater does miracles for your eyes."

"Stop trying to distract me." Carissa's nervousness was making her jumpy.

"Is it that obvious?"

"Everything about you is obvious."

"Oh, yeah," Julie grinned. "I keep forgetting. But seriously, kid, this is the best way. Thumb your nose at Glen. Show him that it doesn't matter. Show him that you're just as good as his perky pom-pom girl. Trust me. With my help, you'll attract boys like honey attracts flies."

"Oh, Julie, if only I had a third of your confidence."

Julie smiled. "Well, it's easy to be confident about you. After all, you've got everything it takes to be really popular."

"Well, I'll need lots of help if I'm going to attract another guy. Especially before the Valentine Ball. I don't even know what it means to flirt!"

"We'll start slow," Julie assured her. "One day at a time. You'll be fine."

Carissa took a deep breath. Glen Matlock was the only boy she'd ever loved. His deception hurt so much. Could she even act outgoing while she was half-dead inside? Well, she could try.

She turned to Julie. "What do I do, Jules?"

"Girls! I'm glad you're here. We're ready to begin." Mr. Reinhardt, the junior class advisor, stood in the doorway waving them in.

Carissa cast Julie a panicked glance. Julie gave her a thumbs-up sign and sauntered into the room. Carissa slunk after her. No time for strategy. She was on her own.

The room was packed. Most of the girls had planted themselves at the long center tables. The boys sprawled on sewing-machine benches on the far side of the room. The

back table had obviously been designated couples only, since it was filled with the junior
class's most prominent steadies. Glen and
Tina were sitting there, Carissa noticed with
a sinking heart.

Julie squeezed through the crowd to a chair
near the line of boys.

Nervous as she was, Carissa had to smile.
Good old Julie, always making sure there was
a guy nearby. Following Julie's lead, Carissa
slid onto an empty bench in the corner, far
away from the table of girls. But it wasn't
because she wanted to be near the guys. It
was the most inconspicuous seat left.

The hairs on the back of her neck began to
crawl. She had the feeling that someone was
staring at her. She looked up in time to see
Glen turn his head away.

He didn't expect me to come, she thought.
He thought I'd chicken out if he didn't bring
me. A feeling of triumph shot through her.
She was proud of herself. Then she noticed
Tina Walters watching. With a proprietary
air, Tina slid her hand around Glen's arm
and inched herself closer to his side.

Carissa's feeling of triumph faded. If she
hadn't sat so far from the door, she could
have escaped. But the door was on the other

side of the room, and there were three tables full of people in the way. She was trapped.

"I'm delighted to see so many of you," Mr. Reinhardt began. "Most of our steering committee is here, and I've asked several others to help us with ideas." He dug into a pile of papers. "I've got some catalogs for you to look at and—"

The school secretary's voice broke over the intercom. "Will Mr. Reinhardt please come to the office for a telephone call?"

"Can't it wait? We're having a meeting."

"It's long-distance, sir."

Mr. Reinhardt gave an impatient grimace. "Very well." He turned toward the group. "Just glance at these until I get back."

As soon as he left the room, there was a buzz of conversation.

"Look at this! We can order a real fountain for the middle of the dance floor."

"Are you planning to dance or swim?"

"Here's a bridge. Maybe we could . . ."

Carissa thought she might die. Why had she ever thought this could work? She shut her eyes. How could she sit there and watch Tina Walters practically climb over Glen? And how could he sit there and look like he enjoyed it? Didn't he have any consideration for her feelings?

A wave of nausea overtook her and she grabbed for the jacket she'd thrown over her chair. But Julie's eyes stopped her.

"Don't you dare," they commanded. Carissa sank backward. How could she ever show Glen anything if she acted like a scared rabbit? That was exactly what he'd disliked in her. But how was she supposed to act instead?

She glanced to her right. Tom Edwards, the center for the Ridgewood basketball team, sat slouched in his seat, half-asleep. To her left was a boy named Ziggy. Ziggy wasn't one of the most attractive boys at Ridgewood, but he had always spoken to her when they met in the halls. She noticed now that his Adam's apple was bobbing, and he wove his fingers together nervously as he sat waiting for Mr. Reinhardt's return.

Ziggy was as nervous as she was! The thought struck her with the force of a blow. He looked as miserable and as out of place as she felt. Relief washed through her. Here was someone she could understand, maybe even help. Perhaps she could forget her own misery if she concentrated on Ziggy's.

She gave him a tentative smile. "Hi, Zig."

He rewarded her with a friendly grin. "Hi."

"What a circus, huh?" What an inane comment, she thought to herself, but he didn't seem to mind.

"Yeah. I must have been crazy to come."

She searched for conversation. "Are you interested in the Valentine Ball?"

"Not really. But I'm *very* interested in the Grass Roots. I thought maybe I could get on a committee to help them set up or something. I'd give anything to do that."

"You're a music buff?"

"Yeah. I want to find out how they made it to the big time. I've been working with a band, doing their lighting, for over a year now." He grinned proudly. "They even let me sing and play a little bit. Anyway, I think we're good. I thought maybe the Grass Roots could give me some advice."

"I'm impressed," Carissa said sincerely. "I didn't know you wanted to be a professional musician." It was fascinating to think of Ziggy in that way. But really, it shouldn't have surprised her. When he walked, Ziggy had the natural rhythm of a born musician. "Tell me about your band."

Zig launched into a detailed account and

Carissa was disappointed when Mr. Reinhardt returned. She'd never known there was so much to organizing a band.

Impulsively she leaned forward and put her hand on Ziggy's arm. "Thanks for the music lesson. I'd like to hear the rest of it later."

Zig nodded eagerly and gave her a wide smile. "Later," he whispered.

As Carissa shifted to face Mr. Reinhardt again, she caught the surprised expression on Glen's face. Coolly she allowed her gaze to cross his face before it settled on the advisor. If Julie was right, what Glen needed most was a little lesson on who Carissa Stevens really was—or, at least, who she could be.

"Before we assign committees—decorations, band, food, etcetera—I'd like suggestions for a theme." Mr. Reinhardt picked up a piece of chalk. "Ideas, anyone?"

"Motorcycle Magic," Rick Schumacher, a bike buff, yelled.

"How about A Night in Paris?" one of the girls suggested.

"Over the Rainbow," Julie piped up. "We could have pots of gold and multicolored streamers and . . ."

". . . and Munchkins," Tom Edwards finished.

Julie shot Tom a deprecating glance. There

was an electricity between Tom and Julie that Carissa had never understood. They seemed to like each other, yet they were constantly sparring with each other.

Before Julie could reply, a low voice came from the doorway. "How about a Valentine Masquerade?"

Carissa gazed at the handsome stranger in the doorway. How long had he been standing there? When the boy realized he had the attention of everyone in the room, he continued.

"Just use three colors—red, black, and silver. Red takes care of the Valentine part. Black and silver can be the mystery of the masquerade. And"—he grinned widely, displaying a row of even white teeth—"I happen to know that the Grass Roots just got new costumes. Black and silver."

The entire room broke into excited chatter. The idea had struck a chord, no doubt about that. But Carissa couldn't seem to get involved in the discussion. Instead she stared at the boy in the doorway. His hair was dark brown, the color of rich milk chocolate, and it matched his eyes. Like most of the guys in the room, he wore jeans and a sweatshirt— but somehow he gave the impression of being dressed in a suit and tie. Carissa had a hard time pulling her gaze away.

"It's a great idea, don't you think," Zig was saying. "Every year the junior class has a big fight over the Valentine theme. Maybe this year we can get right to work and make it the best dance ever!"

"Who's *that*?" Carissa whispered, too engrossed in the new boy to reply to Zig's suggestion.

"Him? That's Rafe Kelton."

"And who is Rafe Kelton?"

Zig grinned. "I thought every female in Ridgewood knew that."

"I guess I'm not like every other female," Carissa retorted, forgetting her shyness.

"Yeah. I can see that."

Zig's words brought her up short. Carissa blushed. What did he mean by that?

"Hey! I meant it as a compliment," Zig hurried to say. He tipped his head to one side in an endearing way. "No other female at Ridgewood has ever talked to me, so I *know* you're different."

"Come off it, Zig."

"No kidding. No one talks to me unless they want something—girls at least."

Carissa's eyes clouded. "I can identify with

that. It's happened to me." Glen's face filled her thoughts. "But it's their loss, Zig."

Now it was Zig's turn to blush.

Carissa had a wild thought: her first stab at talking to boys, and she'd already made a guy blush. Julie would be proud.

"You still didn't answer my question," she persisted. "Who's Rafe Kelton?"

"His family moved here this past summer. Where have you been all year?"

In Glen's arms. Carissa stared even harder at Rafe. Apparently there were some things she'd missed by being so star-struck by Glen.

"He's not around a lot," Zig was explaining. "He's busy after school. Lots of girls wish he stuck around. Now me, I'm always here, but they don't seem to care." Zig grinned and shrugged.

Carissa smiled at Zig. She liked his humor but wished he wouldn't always turn it on himself. He seemed more special than he gave himself credit for. She was suddenly very grateful that she'd chosen this seat. Zig had helped her get through this first outing without Glen.

Mr. Reinhardt was still trying to make some headway with the group. "Any other suggestions for a theme?"

Julie, who was never shy, stood up and

said in a strong voice, "I think a Valentine Masquerade is a great theme. Let's vote on it. Everybody in favor . . ." She stuck her hand high in the air. Soon a roomful of waving hands joined hers.

Mr. Reinhardt looked relieved. "Well, that was easy enough. If you aren't on the steering committee just sign up on the sheets labeled Food, Decorations, Band, etcetera, and you may leave. The chairman of your group will contact you about work schedules . . ." He didn't finish because of the rush toward the sign-up sheets.

Zig whispered in Carissa's ear, "Which committee do you want to be on?"

"Decorations, I think," she whispered back. "Red and black and silver. Sounds nice."

"I hope I get assigned to the band," Zig said wistfully.

The room was emptying out. Rafe had taken a seat at the far end of the room. That meant he was on the steering committee, too. Carissa gazed around the room.

Just then, Glen raised his hand. "Mr. Reinhardt," he began. His face flushed pink, as if he were embarrassed. "Tina would like to volunteer for the steering committee too, if it's all right. She could be my assistant."

Julie spun around in her chair to face Carissa and mouthed the letters "J . . . E . . . R . . . K . . ."

Carissa felt tears rising. She was mortified. How could Glen do this to her? Break up with her one day and then announce to everyone that he wanted Tina to be his assistant?

Ziggy leaned forward. "I'll nominate you for decorations, if you'll put in a good word for me about working with the band." He looked so worried that Carissa managed to stop her tears.

"Sure, Zig. No problem." She gave him a grin, and from the corner of her eye she saw Glen looking puzzled again. Suddenly all her urge to cry was gone. Crying would only remind Glen of the timid little doormouse she'd been. She would prove to him that Tina wasn't the only interesting girl around!

Chapter Three

"It's perfect," Julie gushed on the way home from the meeting. "Everyone got the committee they wanted! Ziggy is in charge of the band, you're heading decorations, and Tom and I are doing publicity." She chuckled drily. "Of course, Glen and Tina got the food and punch committee, and that's what they deserve, the—"

"Jerks. I know. You don't have to say it again."

"You did great, Carissa. I watched you—you knocked Glen's socks off, the way you handled yourself. You and Ziggy kept getting into these deep conversations like you were really having fun. . . ."

"We *were* having fun. Zig is a great guy."

"So what's your plan for the decorations?"

27

Julie switched subjects with a grin. "What kind of a backdrop are you going to use?"

"I think I'd better wait and talk to the rest of my committee about that," Carissa murmured. What had she gotten herself into? She didn't know a thing about backdrops! Her stomach churned nervously. "I'm not sure I can handle all this."

"But you've got a co-chairman," Julie pointed out.

"I do?"

"Didn't you hear Mr. Reinhardt . . . ? Oh, that must have happened when you went to get the streamer samples from the storeroom. Rafe Kelton is your co-chairman."

"Rafe Kelton? Why would he want to make decorations?" She could still see him lounging in the doorway.

"I don't know. Maybe he's artistic. Maybe he likes things like that. After all, he came up with the idea. Uh-oh. Look out."

Carissa glanced up just as Glen came around the corner. Tina was clinging to his arm like a vine.

There was no time to think or to dodge into a doorway to avoid meeting him face-to-face.

"Hi, Cari, Julie." Glen glanced from one to the other with a wary look in his eye.

28

With good reason, too, Carissa thought. He'd called her Cari, his own pet name for her. Why had he reminded her of what they'd had together? Of what she'd lost?

"Come *on*, Glen. We've got to hurry or we'll be late." Tina tugged impatiently on his arm. "The game starts at six-fifteen."

"Hurry, Glen, we'll be late," Julie mimicked as soon as the pair turned the corner. "She sure rubs it in that she's in charge now. He's the biggest sap that—Carissa, are you crying?"

"No. Yes. I don't know." Carissa's eyes brimmed with tears. "It just makes me so *mad*."

"Mad is good. You're better off mad than sad," Julie said firmly. "You're headed in the right direction." She brightened. "Look at it this way—you've totally confused Glen. First you came to the meeting when he never expected you to show up. Then you and Zig carried on this constant conversation. And then, best of all, you're on the decorations committee with Rafe Kelton. I'd call that progress, for the first day after a breakup."

"Some progress," Carissa muttered. "You dragged me to the meeting, Zig is easy to talk to, and I'm on a committee with a boy I've never met. That makes me feel really confident."

"You'll be fine. Rafe's a real hunk. And he marches to his own drummer."

"What's that got to do with me?"

Julie gave her a sly smile. "Nothing—yet."

Carissa sighed as she turned off at her street corner and trudged through the snow toward home. It was one thing for Julie to talk about switching loyalties, but she'd loved Glen for a long time. Even a hunk like Rafe Kelton couldn't change that.

"Got a minute, Carissa? There are some things I'd like to discuss with you."

Grumpily Carissa closed her psychology textbook. She hated to be interrupted when she was studying, unless it was something really important. Her eyes widened in surprise when she looked up. It was Rafe Kelton.

She hadn't seen him since the organizational meeting for the dance. In fact, Carissa had wondered if she'd imagined the whole night. It almost seemed like a dream—and where Glen was concerned, a bad dream.

"I've done some sketches on decorating the gym. Do you have time to look at them?"

Mrs. Olleson, the librarian, was giving them her best dirty looks. Carissa gathered her notebooks. "Sure. Let's go to the room across

the hall. It's empty this period." Mr. Reinhardt had designated it as headquarters for
the Valentine Ball.

Rafe followed her out of the library. When
Carissa saw a couple of Glen's friends watching, she straightened her back and thrust
her chin forward, trying to look nonchalant.

The room was empty, and Rafe kicked the
door shut behind them with the toe of his
boot. Carissa felt nervous suddenly, but she
laughed at herself. She'd been so jumpy lately.

Rafe walked to the long table at the back of
the room. As he spread his sketches on the
table, Carissa studied him.

Rafe had a different look from most of the
boys at Ridgewood. He seemed more mature,
despite his jeans, the short-sleeved shirt which
revealed muscular arms, and his boots, which
seemed to be his trademark. The only guys
around school who wore boots rode motorcy-
cles, and none of their footwear was quite
like Rafe's. And Rafe Kelton couldn't seem to
walk without swaggering.

"Well, what do you think?"

His question startled her. Slowly she walked
toward the table.

Where's Julie when I really need her, she
wondered. What was she supposed to say?

She felt like a rabbit being eyed by a panther. A wave of shyness made her duck her head.

"Even if you don't like them, I won't bite." His tone was amused.

Carissa gave him a startled glance.

"Don't look so scared. They're just pictures."

She blushed so hard she could feel her neck grow warm. No one had ever confronted her shyness so directly, especially not a virtual stranger. But her discomfort disappeared as she stared at the designs on the table.

"These are wonderful!" she told him, smiling.

Rafe had drawn a circular dance floor. One side of the circle was open with a second circle jutting into it. That was the band's platform. Around the perimeter of the room he'd drawn tall, graceful columns. At the top of each column was a huge mask with streamers dangling down each side. The masks were all slightly different. Together they gave the effect of watching the dance floor.

"There are some columns left over from another dance," he explained. "Mr. Reinhardt asked if we could use them in any way, to cut down on expenses. They're already silver. If we make the masks black and red with streamers in all three colors draping down the sides, I think we can create a good effect."

"It's incredible, Rafe. These sketches are beautiful."

"I don't know about beautiful, but they give you an idea of what I'm talking about. There's black poly sheeting available too. That will create a good background. Cover the bleachers in the gym, anyway." He stopped for a moment, looking embarrassed. "Sorry. You probably have a dozen ideas and I'm just babbling on about mine."

"Don't stop!" Carissa was surprised by the excitement she felt looking at the drawings. "This is better than anything I could come up with." She stared at him in frank admiration, her shyness momentarily forgotten. "You're a wonderful artist."

He smiled. "Thanks. I'll keep working on it then."

Carissa picked up the nearest drawing and studied it carefully. He'd worked long and hard on this picture. All the darkened areas were neatly crosshatched, and every line was in place. She could almost see herself on the ballroom floor. . . .

Coming back to reality with a jolt, she dropped the page onto the table. She wasn't going to be at the dance. Tina Walters had seen to that.

"Something wrong?" Rafe always seemed to get right to the point.

"No," Carissa lied. "I was just thinking . . . wouldn't it be great to have helium balloons floating around? They could be red and black and silver Mylar."

"Or we could attach long ribbons to them and tie a weight at the end so they hovered."

"Or we could let a few go to the ceiling . . ."

". . . like stars?"

She clapped her hands together with delight. "Exactly! Just like stars!"

The door opened, and Ziggy flew into the room, the laces of his high-tops clicking on the tile. "Hey, Rafe! There you are! There's a call for you in the office. The secretary's paging you. The loudspeaker must be off in this room."

Rafe turned to Carissa. "Excuse me?"

When Carissa nodded, he gathered up his drawings and stuffed them carelessly into a notebook. If she'd created masterpieces like those, Carissa thought, she would put them under glass. But Rafe acted as if there were a million more where those came from.

"Hey, Carissa!" Zig finally realized that she was in the room.

"Hi, Zig. How's the band?"

He looked so pleased that she'd asked that Carissa felt a flush of pleasure. "Great. Just great. Thanks for asking."

Carissa smiled as the two bolted from the room, Rafe in the lead, Zig a step behind. Somehow Ziggy made her forget her own shyness. He almost seemed more timid than she was.

Carissa perched on the edge of the table and chewed on the end of her pencil. Rafe Kelton was interesting, too, in a different way. She would have expected a boy who looked like him—handsome and so sure of himself —to be tough. But he was artistic and mysterious. He couldn't have been around much if this week was the first time she'd seen him. Where had Rafe Kelton been? And why had he entered her life now? It was an interesting question, but glancing at her watch she realized this was no time to think about it. She was late for her next class!

"Going to today's meeting, Carissa? I can't believe there's only a couple of weeks to get things done. I'm so excited. Aren't you?" Julie certainly looked pleased about it.

Carissa gave her a wry look. "Should I be excited about the fact that I'm working like crazy for a dance I'm not going to? Or about attending meetings where Tina Walters crawls all over Glen?"

"Oh, forget about Glen!" Julie frowned. "He's not worth the trouble. If he's too dumb to know a good thing when he has it . . ."

Julie launched into one of her sermons about Glen Matlock's innate stupidity. Carissa grinned; she'd heard Julie lecture on Glen's shortcomings many times since their breakup.

She was hardly looking forward to another committee meeting—Glen and Tina always sat so close together that it was almost more than she could bear. Thank goodness for Zig and Julie. They kept her too busy to think about Glen.

Still, Carissa mused as Julie chatted on, the meetings were kind of fun. She'd met more people in the last few days than she had in her entire sophomore year of school. Even Tom Edwards, the basketball center, had begun saying hello to her in the hallways. And, better yet, she'd managed to smile and return his greetings.

". . . do you think he will, Carissa? He's missed so many."

"What?" Carissa realized that Julie was asking her a question.

"Do you think Rafe Kelton will be at the meeting? He's sure missed a lot of them. I think Mr. Reinhardt would be upset about it except that Rafe keeps turning in those beautiful sketches. Plus you two have the decorations more organized than they've ever been before."

"You mean that Rafe has them organized. I've hardly done a thing. I just go gaga over his drawings and he sets everything up."

Julie shot her a teasing look. "Are you sure it's not Rafe you're going gaga over?"

Carissa gave her a withering look. "Hardly. Anyway, he's not interested in me."

"Just a thought." Julie grinned. "After all, he's awfully cute, and the dance is getting closer. And you've been *very* friendly."

"Like you said," Carissa reminded her, "that's to show Glen what he's missing."

Carissa was thankful to see the home ec room come into sight. It was harder and harder to think of staying home from the dance now that she'd become so involved, but she wasn't going to get her hopes up.

She could tick off all the boys she knew—and was brave enough to talk to—on one hand: Ziggy, who, Carissa had discovered, had a girlfriend in a neighboring school district; Tom Edwards, who'd finally perked up enough in one of the committee meetings to notice Julie and ask her out on a date; and Rafe, who was still a mystery to her.

On several occasions, Carissa had seen him leave school immediately after the final bell. He never stayed to talk to anyone, and he seemed completely uninvolved with extracurricular activities—other than the Valentine Masquerade. Once she'd seen a youthful-looking woman in a silver-gray Audi pick him up. They'd driven away together.

Could Rafe be dating an older woman? That could make him mysterious and aloof. And it would explain the pretty young woman in the expensive car.

Carissa sighed. None of this would help her get a date.

Ziggy, Tom, and Rafe were the only guys she knew. Unless, of course, you counted Glen.

"Hi, Carissa."

It was all she could do to keep from gasping out loud when she heard Glen's voice.

Somehow she controlled herself and stammered a hello.

"Jerk," Julie hissed in her ear before floating off to meet Tom.

Carissa stared at Julie's back for a moment before turning to Glen.

"Uh—ready for the meeting?" she asked him.

"Sure. And you?"

"I suppose so." Why was he talking to her? Had Tina retracted her claws and let him get away?

"Sounds like it's going to be great." He threw his head back with a cocky air.

"Yes." Here it was, the moment she'd waited for—Glen, alone with her. And she couldn't think of a thing to say. Side by side, they walked to the classroom.

Carissa could hear the buzz of conversation inside and Mr. Reinhardt trying to get some order, but Glen hesitated at the door, his gaze fixed on her face.

"What's the deal with you, Carissa?"

"Deal? With me?" Why did her voice have to squeak like that when she was nervous? "There's no deal with me."

"Yeah? I never expected *you* to be on the Valentine committee."

39

"We volunteered together, Glen, *remember?*"

"I know, but after . . . I thought you'd—"

"You thought I couldn't do it?"

"You surprised me, that's all. No big deal."

Julie had been right. Glen didn't believe shy Carissa had any spunk. He'd wanted someone he could show off, someone flashy. Someone like the person Carissa was pretending to be.

A war was raging within her. Part of her wanted to run. To be herself—shy and quiet. But she had to show Glen she could stand on her own two feet. She would show him she had what it took.

With a flick of her long blond hair, Carissa eyed him coolly—just like the movie stars she'd seen on late-night TV. "I'm full of surprises, Glen. Too bad you didn't take the time to discover what they were." And with another swing of her hair, Carissa managed to pivot and glide into the meeting room, leaving Glen in the hallway, his mouth open in surprise.

By the time she got to her seat, Carissa's legs were wobbly. She took a deep breath and sank gratefully into her chair.

She'd done it! It hadn't been as difficult as she'd imagined, standing up to Glen. Tina was looking at her in surprise, and Julie caught her eye, nodding approval.

Feeling better than she had in days, Carissa turned toward Ziggy and gave him a dazzling smile and a huge, theatrical wink. This was fun, she realized. Acting like someone else made her feel like someone else—like a perky, outgoing Carissa. Someone fun to be with. Someone a boy like Glen would be proud to date. Or at least, someone she was proud to be!

Chapter Four

What if I could get him back? Carissa suddenly stood stock-still. Julie bumped into her from behind as the two pushed through the crowded halls toward their lockers.

After seeing the look in Glen's eyes at the meeting the day before, Carissa thought it was a real possibility. Since then, he'd been showing an unusual interest in her. And she was feeling more and more outgoing, especially with friends, and Ziggy. Of course, it was easy to be carefree with Ziggy because he was so open to her attention. And what little talking she'd done with Rafe was easy, too—but then, he was so businesslike and mature.

Being around Rafe was almost like being around Mr. Reinhardt. Maybe that came with dating older women, Carissa mused—if that's what Rafe actually did. She'd heard lots of theories about why he didn't take part in school activities. Around school, he was a mystery man.

"What are you thinking about?" Julie asked. "You look like you're a million miles away."

"Guys," Carissa admitted as she threw her books into her locker. These days, she was taking less work home. Glen had always said she practiced 'overkill' with her assignments, and she'd finally decided he was right.

"Yeah, me too." Julie had a self-satisfied expression on her face. Sighing dreamily, she leaned against her locker. "Tom asked me to the Valentine Masquerade today."

"Jules!" Carissa squealed. "You fox!"

"I know. Isn't it great? He's such a hunk. Nice, too. Want to help me find a new dress?"

"Of course. Something blue to go with your eyes."

"And slinky to go with my bod?"

Carissa giggled. "Why not?"

Julie snorted. "Who are we kidding? You're the slinky one in this duo. You know, you'd be great in a low-cut—"

"Bathrobe? That's probably all I'm going to need on Valentine's Day."

Julie rolled her eyes. "You haven't given up on getting a date, have you? Why? You're doing great. Just flirt a little more. There are dozens of guys without dates. What about Zig? He thinks you're the greatest thing since sliced bread."

"He already has a girlfriend. Besides, Zig and I are just friends."

"Well, Tom wouldn't mind double-dating if you want to come with us. All we need now is a boy."

"Well, it's not like going to a delicatessen and picking out sandwiches, so don't get your hopes up," Carissa instructed her friend. Secretly, she wondered if Glen would ask her after all.

Even though Glen managed to find one reason or another to ask her a question or just say hello, Tina was usually locked to his arm like a pair of handcuffs. He'd probably already made plans with Tina for the dance. Carissa sighed. The more she worked on planning the dance, the more she wanted to go.

"Why so sad?"

The voice was not Julie's. It wasn't even female. And it sent a surprising shiver down Carissa's spine.

44

"Rafe!"

"Something wrong?" His tone was warm, as if it really mattered to him.

"No, not really."

"You look as if you'd lost your best friend."

"Not at all." Carissa flushed. "Maybe I'm just tired. Last night I had nightmares—we hadn't ordered enough streamers or balloons or anything. We had to decorate with what we had and ended up with a dance floor the size of a tabletop."

Rafe threw back his head and roared with laughter. He grinned at her. "Last night I dreamed that we'd ordered too *much* stuff, and we decorated every room in the school. Then Mr. Reinhardt decided we had to pay for all the extras out of our own pockets. I spent half the night trying to find a part-time job that paid a hundred dollars an hour!"

Julie, who was discreetly sorting through a stack of papers at her locker, glanced up. She gave Carissa a curious look.

Carissa swung around so her back was to her friend. "Actually, I rechecked all the figures this morning. We should be okay. Mr. Reinhardt expects the supplies today or tomorrow."

Rafe smiled. "I know. I checked, too. Powerful dreams we have." His gaze lingered on her face.

Carissa wondered if there was a double meaning to his statement—one she didn't understand. Inexperience with men was no blessing, she decided. She didn't know what to say next, though. Rafe seemed perfectly comfortable standing there, staring at her with those dark brown eyes that seemed to see everything.

"Maybe . . . maybe I'd better get going," she finally stammered.

"Going where?"

"Just home."

"No where else?"

"N-no."

"Do you have time to stop at Andre's?"

Andre's was a little coffee shop about three blocks from the school. From three until five it was a hangout for steady couples and any students flush with pocket money. After five, it turned into a trendy French restaurant. Everyone who went to Andre's usually fulfilled one of two requirements: either they were part of a steady couple who liked the dark private booths that lined the walls, or they were willing to pay high prices for flavored mineral water or cappuccino. Glen had never taken Carissa to Andre's.

Just as she was about to refuse—what would she say to this boy she hardly knew—a sharp pain shot through her ankle. Carissa looked down to see the corner of Julie's physics book stabbing her leg.

Muffling a giggle, Carissa said, "I suppose. For a little while."

Julie hoisted her books onto her hip, wagging her fingers in a victory sign. Then, with the flair of Scarlett O'Hara sailing past Rhett Butler in *Gone With the Wind*, she disappeared down the hallway. If Carissa hadn't looked over Rafe's shoulder at just the right moment, she would have missed Julie leaping into the air and clicking her heels together.

"Ready?" Rafe asked her. "I'll have to stop and make a phone call on the way."

Carissa nodded. Rafe hadn't taken his eyes off her. It was rather disconcerting. Glen had never stared at her quite like this. Her heart started to pound. What had she gotten herself into now?

Her tongue and her brain had picked a fine time to go on vacation, Carissa thought woefully. She couldn't talk, and she wouldn't have been able to think of anything to say if she could.

Rafe, however, didn't seem to mind her silence. He sauntered beside her with that cool air that made him seem so mysterious. Carissa began to wonder if she'd made a mistake. Then she saw Ziggy from out of the corner of her eye. He was deep in conversation with a teacher and didn't see her walk by. Still, the sight of him gave her an idea. She would treat Rafe just like she treated Ziggy. So what if Ziggy was shy and awkward while Rafe was confident and smooth? So what if Ziggy was funny-looking and Rafe looked like every girl's dream man? So what if she and Zig related to each other because they sometimes felt like outcasts? Maybe somewhere under Rafe's gorgeous exterior there beat a timid heart?

Carissa remembered what Julie had often told her: "Think about making *him* feel comfortable. Then you'll forget about how nervous you are."

"Do you like French food?" she blurted. It was the first thing that came to her mind as they turned the corner and saw Andre's small brass sign.

Rafe answered politely. "Yes, I do. But I also like Mexican and Chinese."

"What's your favorite? Burritos? Fajitas? Enchiladas? Sweet and sour?" She realized she was babbling. He was going to think she was an idiot!

"Fajitas, I think. Do you like them?"

By the time they'd ordered two cappuccinos, they were talking animatedly about not only food but restaurants and places they'd visited.

Carissa's father believed in taking her to fine restaurants when they traveled, and it sounded as if Rafe had had similar experiences.

"Does your family travel much, Rafe?" By the sudden change of his expression, she wondered if it had been too personal a question.

Seeing that he didn't want to continue, she quickly changed the subject. He obviously didn't want to talk about his family.

Her plan seemed to work, and it was a shock when she glanced at her wristwatch. "It's nearly five! I didn't realize how late it was getting." She gathered up her books and searched the booth for her gloves. "I promised Mom I'd help with supper."

"Here, I'll carry your books," Rafe offered.

"With our long legs, we'll be at your house in no time."

She glanced at him shyly. "I really appreciate this. Thank you."

Rafe tipped his head briefly, but he didn't speak.

Somehow, Carissa was disappointed. He could have said, "Sure, anytime," or given some clue that he wanted to see her again, but he didn't. But he took her arm and steered her out of Andre's and into the softly falling snow.

There were few things that made Carissa forget how self-conscious she was, but freshly falling snow was one of them. She turned her face to the sky and closed her eyes. Puffy flakes fell on her eyelashes and nose. Impulsively she stuck out her tongue and caught a flake on its tip. As she whirled around with her arms outstretched, the white cover crunched beneath her boots. "I just love snow!"

Rafe's chuckle brought her back to the present. "I can see that."

She felt a blush spread from ear to ear. "Sorry. I'm usually not so . . . strange."

"That's okay. I like it."

She glanced at him from out of the corner

of her eye. He actually seemed to mean it! Glen would have told her to quit being weird.

"This is it," Carissa announced as they reached her split-level house. She marched to the door before turning to face Rafe. All she could manage was a gruff, "Thank you."

"Thank *you*," he answered. Rafe stood on her doorstep, his hands buried deep in his pockets, his brown eyes smiling.

"Good night." She turned to make a quick escape, but the door knob didn't turn. Oh, great! She was either going to have to ring the bell or make her way through the garage.

"I guess I have to go in the other—"

"Carissa." His tone stopped her dead in her tracks. She looked at him questioningly.

"You realize, don't you, that I still don't know anything about you? We spent the entire afternoon talking about *my* favorite foods and books and movies. . . ."

"I'm sorry. I was just . . ."

"Don't apologize. Just offer to do something about it." His eyes were dancing with mischief.

"But what can I do? I guess I could—"

"Go out with me on Friday night? Give me a chance to ask *you* some questions. Deal?"

"D—deal."

"Great! G'night, Carissa. See you at seven on Friday."

She stared at the tracks his feet made in the snow just to reassure herself that he had actually been there, standing on her step, asking her out.

Asking her out! Carissa sucked in a huge, gulping breath of cold air. He'd asked her out, and she'd accepted! Wait until Julie got word of this!"

Chapter Five

Carissa didn't see Rafe at school on Tuesday or Wednesday. On Thursday she caught a glimpse of him hurrying home from school while the last bell was still chiming. By Friday she'd given up on ever talking to him.

The hours at Andre's must have been a figment of her imagination. The cappuccino, the snow, Rafe's smile . . .

Julie jarred her out of her thoughts.

"Where does he go, anyway?"

Carissa blinked, her green eyes still vacant and dreamy. "Who?"

"Rafe Kelton, of course. We were in study hall last hour and all of a sudden he looked at his watch and shot out of his chair like a cannonball. The bell rang, and before I got my books together he was running across the lawn. He jumped into the big silver car and drove away.

"I don't know, Jules. I have no idea where he goes after school."

"You were out with him. Didn't you ask?"

"No."

"How'd I ever hook up with an uncurious creature like you?" Julie chided. "You are absolutely no good at gossip. Except of course"—Julie's smile turned impish—"for the fact that you've got a date with Mr. Mystery himself."

"You haven't told anyone, have you?" Carissa felt alarmed.

"No. You swore me to secrecy, remember? Why, I'll never know. If I were going out with a hunk like that I'd shout it from the— "

"I'm not sure we *are* going out."

"Huh?" Julie paused. "Why do you say that?"

Carissa shrugged. "He hasn't talked to me all week. He wasn't at any of our meetings. Even Mr. Reinhardt wondered where he was. I'm beginning to think I imagined the whole thing."

"You? Miss Feet-on-the-ground Stevens? Not a chance." Julie turned thoughtful. "Rafe's family just moved here. No one seems to know much about him." She looked a little sheepish. "He's always intimidated me. He seems so wise and mature. I guess that's why he's attracted to you."

"Huh?"

"Sure. Because you seem older, too. It's hard to explain, but—" Julie's brows knit in thought. "It's like he's got responsibility or something." She flicked her hair away from her face. "He doesn't act like a crazy kid without a care in the world."

Maybe that's what she liked about him. Carissa mused. She'd never felt as carefree and happy-go-lucky as Julie. She'd always felt like a stick-in-the-mud compared to the giggly girls she knew. Even Glen had chided her, telling her to lighten up. But with Rafe, she never felt as though she were too serious. She smiled to herself. Perhaps that's why she hadn't felt shy with him either—he accepted her as she was, not as she wished she could be.

As they walked toward their lockers, Julie asked, "So what are you wearing tonight? Tell me all."

"I told you—I haven't talked to Rafe all week. I'm not sure that our date is on."

"Ridiculous! Rafe Kelton never stands up a date!"

"Do you know that for sure?" Carissa stared hard at Julie.

"Well . . . not exactly. I don't know anyone he's ever dated." She brightened. "But he doesn't seem the type."

True, Carissa thought. He *didn't* seem the type to disappoint someone.

"What type is he, then?" Carissa asked aloud.

"Strong, dark, sexy, mysterious . . ."

"There you go again, making it sound like he leads a double life or something."

Julie shrugged. "Don't pay any attention to me. I just heard a curious conversation the other day."

"What was that?"

"Some of the girls were wondering why Rafe doesn't go out for sports. I mean he's got a really good build. That led to where he goes in such a hurry after school."

"And what did they decide?" For some reason it bothered Carissa that other girls were talking about Rafe this way, but she was too curious herself to criticize.

"Nothing. Nobody knows anything about him. The only one he ever seems to spend time with is Ziggy, and Zig is like a clam." Julie gave her friend an impish grin. "So they made up their own theories. Patty Simer thinks he's an undercover narcotics agent."

"Get real!"

"And Wendy Rivers thinks he's got a job and he's been lying about his age to keep it. That's why he doesn't want any school kids to know where he goes."

Carissa rolled her eyes.

"But Amy Laurence had the most interesting idea."

"Oh?"

"Yeah. She says that the woman who picks him up sometimes—the one in the silver Audi—is his girlfriend."

"But that woman is at least thirty!" Carissa stared in surprise, forgetting that she had once thought the same thing. But she'd seen the beautiful dark-haired lady and realized that she was too much older than Rafe to be his girlfriend.

Julie waggled her eyebrows. "Who knows? You're the first girl his own age I've ever heard of him hanging out with. You'll have to find out the answers."

That last comment didn't make Carissa feel any better about the upcoming evening. Rafe was more of an enigma than ever. That would make it even more difficult to explain to her parents about her upcoming date.

"I'm delighted that you're finally getting out and meeting new people, Carissa," her mother said, beaming. "You've been locked up in this house pining about Glen for too long." Mrs. Stevens, a nurse at Ridgewood General, was tall, blond, and slender like her daughter. She moved to her husband's side. "Don't you agree, Mike?"

Carissa's father glanced over the top of the term paper he was reading. He was a professor at the college and seemed to be forever grading papers. "So what's this Romeo's name?"

"Rafe Kelton." Carissa was beginning to regret saying yes. First there was the suspense of wondering whether or not he'd even come, and now the inevitable inquisition by her parents.

"Kelton?" Her father's brow knit in puzzlement. "Where have I heard that name before?"

"Probably a dozen places," Mrs. Stevens assured him. "How unusual can that name be?"

"Kelton, huh? I think I had a student named Kelton."

"Well, I'd better get ready now," Carissa stammered, backing out of the living room. "Just in case he actually comes," she added nervously to herself.

By six-thirty there were a dozen outfits strewn about her bedroom, and Carissa still hadn't decided what to wear.

"Troubles?" her mother asked from the doorway.

"I don't know where we're going or what we're doing or even if he's coming! How can I pick an outfit when . . ."

"Calm down." Mrs. Stevens chuckled. "First things first. Do you want to wear a dress or pants?"

"A dress. No, pants. Well, maybe . . ."

"Go with your instincts."

"A dress, then," Carissa sighed. "He seems like the type that might appreciate a girl who dressed up."

"Good. I like him already." Her mother smiled. "Now then, dressy or casual?"

By six forty-five, Carissa was pacing the floor in front of the fireplace in a mint green denim skirt and matching sweater. Not too dressy, not too casual. And the short skirt made the very best of her long, slender legs.

She'd pulled her hair to one side of her head in a ponytail that cascaded over one shoulder. Her mother had allowed her to use a spritz of her best perfume. Even Carissa's father glanced up from his grading to utter an approving "Wow."

By one minute to seven Carissa had reapplied her peach lip gloss three times, retied the ribbon in her hair twice, and rearranged all the hats and gloves in the hall closet.

"He's not coming. I should have known. Maybe Glen was right. I can't keep a guy. I can't even *get* a—" Her frantic murmuring was cut short by the sound of the doorbell.

Mrs. Stevens faded discreetly into the kitchen after making a shooing motion at her daughter to open the door. The bell rang again.

Carissa opened it to find Rafe standing casually in the doorway, his head tipped appealingly to one side, his hand resting in the pocket of his jacket.

Rafe stamped the snow off his highly polished boots and stepped inside.

He seemed even better-looking than she'd remembered. His dark hair glistened with flecks of melting snow, and his cheeks were bright with cold. As he rubbed his hands together to warm them, she admired his broad shoulders. His eyes were as deep and dark as midnight, and they sparkled.

"You look great," Rafe told her.

Carissa thought of her struggle to get her outfit together and smiled. "Thank you. So do you."

When Carissa realized what she had said, she blushed. If the floor opened up at that moment, she would have willingly sunk through it. "I mean, you look nice. I mean, nice jacket, I mean . . ."

"It's okay. Guys like a compliment now and then, too, you know." He grinned and moved into the foyer, radiating ease and confidence.

Mr. Stevens rose to meet Carissa's date. Rather than being awkward and ill at ease, as Glen had been each and every time he had to talk to her father, Rafe simply offered a friendly hand in greeting. Before Carissa knew what was happening, Mr. Stevens was showing Rafe the boat he was building inside a large bottle, and Rafe was enthusiastically admiring the work in progress.

Finally, after a few minutes, Carissa simply took her coat from the closet and put it on.

Rafe looked up with a sheepish smile. "Ready? Sorry. Your father's project is very interesting."

Much to Carissa's amazement, Mr. Stevens flung his arm around Rafe's shoulders as he walked him over to the front hallway. "You'll have to come back and see it when I've finished. Maybe . . ."

How does he do *that,* she wondered. Her

father was talking to her date as if he were one of the professors at the college. What was it about Rafe that inspired such confidence from an adult like her father? She remembered noticing that teachers at school treated him in a similar way.

When they finally escaped into the snow, Carissa half expected to see the mysterious silver car sitting in front of the house. Instead, there was a little black Fiero. She smiled to herself. It was exactly the kind of car she imagined Rafe driving.

As she slid inside, the smell of leather mixed with the smell of wool damp from the snow. And Rafe's shaving lotion had filled the car with a warm and heady scent. Carissa breathed deeply.

He slid in beside her. "All ready?" The car was so small that when he placed his black-gloved hand on the stick shift his knuckles grazed her arm.

"Where are we going?"

Rafe smiled at her. In the dim light, his features took on striking planes. Carissa felt as if she were living out a fantasy: a date with a dream man.

"I thought I'd let you help me decide. Have you eaten?"

"Not much." Truthfully, her stomach had been too nervous to swallow a bit of her mother's dinner.

"There's a show at the Brewer Art Gallery," he began. "There's also a production at the community theater that still has rush seats available, and"—he grinned impishly—"there's a band at the Teen Center on Third Street."

The Brewer Gallery! It was Carissa's favorite place in all of Ridgewood. But would a seventeen-year-old boy actually want to take a girl to an art gallery when there was a band playing somewhere? Maybe he was just being nice, giving her a choice.

"Whatever you want, Rafe."

"Uh-uh. No way. I want you to decide." He touched her arm firmly. "This is *your* night."

Human beings *could* melt, Carissa decided. Her insides had just begun the process. But why? The only boy she'd ever liked was Glen. She still liked Glen, didn't she?

Meanwhile, what would Rafe prefer? The dance, probably. But he was the one who'd brought up the gallery and the theater. . . . Finally, shyly, she spoke. "The dance is just fine, Rafe, if you'd like. Maybe we could stop by the gallery for just a minute though, and . . ."

"The gallery first, dinner second," Rafe said with a decided air. "And *if* we feel like it, we can go to the dance." He turned and stared at her. "Maybe."

Carissa laughed, as a delightful shiver ran through her. "Thank you. I'd *love* to go to the gallery."

Rafe pulled out of the driveway and headed down the street. "From now on, tell me what *you* want when I ask you, not what you think *I* want."

"Yessir," she responded lightly. But her delight at the evening's plans was apparent in her voice.

"After all," Rafe said, his voice easy and friendly, "I'm not afraid to tell you what I want."

Two hours later, after an exhilarating tour of the gallery, Carissa and Rafe were back at Andre's.

"You don't mind eating here, do you? The atmosphere is different in the evening than it is after school."

Carissa gazed happily around the candlelit room. "I love it here. I never thought I'd get to come back."

Rafe looked surprised. "I thought a girl like

64

you would have eaten here a dozen times by now."

A girl like me. Carissa shivered with pleasure.

"No. Not likely. I don't know who would take me."

"One of a hundred guys, I'd think."

Rafe seemed to know exactly the right thing to say. Carissa smiled. If he wanted to think that, it was fine with her. Her actual dating experience didn't make very exciting conversation.

"I don't think you give yourself enough credit, Carissa." His unexpected words caught her by surprise.

She glanced up at him. In the candlelight, his dark eyes gleamed. A lock of dark hair had fallen over his forehead. Only the gleam of his white shirt relieved the darkness in the shadowed booth.

"You're very shy, aren't you?"

"Yes," she admitted ruefully. "No matter how hard I try not to be. I thought I fooled you, though."

"Not really. But I don't mind shyness. Do you want to know what first attracted me to you?" He locked eyes with her. "Well, do you?"

She was taken aback by his frankness. She and Glen in all their months of dating, had never talked so openly as Rafe did in just a few hours.

"Yes. I would." She braced herself for the answer.

"Ziggy."

"What?"

"My friend Ziggy."

"Ziggy made me attractive to you?" She stared in confusion.

Rafe chuckled. "The way you treated Ziggy made me feel attracted to you."

"But Ziggy is a sweetheart. How . . ."

"He's a great guy," Rafe agreed. "But how many girls treat him that way?"

"Well, there's . . ." she paused to consider. Ziggy was very popular with the guys. They appreciated his good humor and unfailing enthusiasm. He was terrible at sports, but eager to support them. Ziggy was the student manager of choice for every team. But the girls . . .

"See what I mean?" Rafe broke into her thoughts. "I watched you at the first meeting for the Valentine Dance. I'd talked Ziggy into going to that meeting, but I was late. I thought I'd have to sit by him and pump him up. By the time I got there, you were talking to him as though he were the most important person in the room."

"But . . ."

"And Ziggy told me later that he wouldn't have made it through that first meeting without you." Rafe gazed into Carissa's eyes. "I wanted to get to know you because you're nice, Carissa Stevens. A really nice person."

Carissa looked down at her folded hands in confusion. At that moment, if she'd had to talk to save her life, she couldn't have done it. She'd never felt quite this way before. Rafe was turning into a wonderful new friend. *Even more than a friend?* she thought and felt herself blushing. Rafe wasn't interested in her that way—or was he? Besides, Glen was the only boy she had ever cared for. . . .

She felt so confused her head was spinning. She still liked Glen, but he didn't ask her out. Rafe asked her out, but only acted like a friend. She didn't understand boys. Would she ever figure things out?

Chapter Six

"Well, welcome back to the real world!"

Carissa blinked. Julie's face was so close to hers that their noses nearly touched.

"Huh?"

"You faded out on me again. One minute you're with me, the next your mind has gone warp-speed into outer space. Are you still thinking about your big date?"

"Come off it, Jules. I just have a lot on my mind."

"This is your best friend in the entire world you're talking to," Julie chided her. "Don't try that kind of nonsense. 'I just have a lot on my mind.' Hah! You only have one thing on your mind. Rafe Kelton!"

"Imagine whatever you want, Jules. It's a free country."

Julie grinned impishly. "Tell me about it. I've been waiting all day to hear."

They were sprawled on the couch in Julie's living room, sodas and bags of chips at their feet.

"It was . . . nice."

" 'Nice?' A 'nice' date wouldn't make you walk on air, Carissa. Where did you go? What did you do?"

"We went to the art gallery. A new show had just gone up and—"

Julie's face flooded with disappointment. "The art gallery? You've got to be kidding!"

"No. It was a great show. Watercolors, oils, collages . . ."

"He took you to an art gallery?" Julie shook her head as if it were too strange to believe.

"And then we went out for dinner. We shared a plate of escargots at Andre's, Jules. I thought it would be gross, but Rafe made me try it. It's not half bad."

"An art show and snails! Whoopee." Julie spun her finger in the air. "What a dumb evening."

"Dumb? It was the most wonderful evening I ever had!"

"Then you and Rafe Kelton are made for each other. Who else would want to do anything like that?"

Carissa had asked herself the same question. She could hardly believe her good luck—Rafe liked the same things she did. He'd picked just the right kind of places to make her feel at home. But that was impossible to explain to Julie, who probably never felt out of place anywhere.

"Well, when are you going to see him again?" Julie had recovered from her disappointment over the odd agenda for their date. "Since you both like things like art shows and snails?"

"I don't know." Carissa felt her spirits dropping.

Rafe had been so attentive and kind on their date that she felt as though he'd surely ask her out again, but when he'd left her at the door—with a gentle kiss on the cheek—he hadn't said anything about another date.

Carissa's frustration mounted with every passing day. Mr. Reinhardt had gotten her excused from her last-hour study hall so she and Rafe had time to construct the silver columns and huge masks that would circle the dance floor.

It was a special time for her. Rafe made her feel so important—so *valued*. He laughed at her jokes and teased when she became too serious, as together they stapled silver rope to the edges of the four-foot masks. Occasionally she would catch him watching when she looked up from her work to push her long hair behind her ears.

Then, at three-thirty, as they cleaned up and put things away, Rafe would turn to her and casually ask, "Andre's?"

If she nodded yes, he would excuse himself to make a phone call, and when he returned, they'd make their way to the little cafe. Usually their booth would be open, waiting for them, just like the regulars who had been coming there after school all year. Yet never once did Rafe suggest attending the Valentine Masquerade together. Carissa had to assume they were only friends. And she still knew practically nothing about him.

"Hi, Carissa. Is your committee ready for the dance?" Glen put his books down next to hers as she sat in the back of the science lab one afternoon.

71

"Sure," she stammered, surprised at his friendly visit. Usually when there was any chance that Tina might pop in, he was very careful not to look as though he enjoyed talking to her. "We're all set to go. Since the dance is a week from Saturday, Mr. Reinhardt said we could begin installing the decorations next Wednesday. How's the food and punch committee doing?"

Glen shrugged. "Okay, I guess. Tina and I have talked about it. No big deal. We'll get it organized soon."

Carissa nodded, wondering if they would get their work done in time. Glen stood awkwardly, shifting his weight from one foot to the other as if he didn't know what to say. It was surprising for Glen to be the nervous one for once. Carissa tried not to smile at the thought.

What was wrong with her, anyway? Three weeks ago she would have died for a chance to be with Glen. Now . . .

"You're looking—good, Carissa," Glen offered at last. "I like your hair that way."

She brushed back the ponytail that fell across her shoulders. She'd been wearing it to one side since her night out with Rafe. "Thanks."

72

"You've been looking . . . different lately. Good, I mean. Real good." Glen's face flushed a bright pink.

"Thanks." She grinned, surprised by this unexpected compliment.

"Yeah, well . . ." He stood up, and his chair scraped against the floor. "Better go. I've got someone to meet."

Tina, no doubt. Carissa nodded. "Sure. See you."

Glen backed slowly toward the door. "Right. Later, maybe. Or tomorrow."

He disappeared backwards through the doorway.

A flicker of excitement ran through Carissa. He'd sought her out. He wanted to talk to her! Carissa thought he was as cute as ever. Still, she hadn't realized before now how awkward Glen could be sometimes. Funny—she'd always been the awkward one before.

A commotion broke out in the hallway—a full-blown fight by the sound of it. Carissa went to investigate.

Maxie Johnson, star quarterback and heavyweight wrestler for Ridgewood High, had obviously decided to massacre someone. Carissa could see a pair of legs lifted six inches off the ground, flailing between Maxie's meaty

73

calves. Whoever Maxie had in his fist was about to get clobbered.

There was something familiar about the victim's scuffed loafers. Ziggy! Maxie had him suspended in midair!

"You're a dumb little twerp, Zig. Do you know that?"

"Put me down, Max." Ziggy's voice had a strangled quality, as if he wasn't getting much air through his windpipe.

"You've just committed suicide, Twerp." Maxie shoved Zig into the wall of lockers, and Ziggy's head bounced painfully off the metal.

A crowd had gathered. Carissa leaned over and whispered to a girl she knew. "What's going on?"

"Maxie's mad."

"I can see that!"

"Zig found cigarettes in his locker and told the coach."

"Oh." Poor Ziggy, Carissa thought. He looked helpless, and completely at Maxie's mercy.

Anxiously, Carissa glanced down the hall. Where was a teacher when you really needed one? Maxie was famous for his flaring temper. He could be mild-mannered as a teddy bear, but when he got mad, he was deadly.

The thud of bones against metal made her wince.

Ziggy's glasses were askew, and the color was gone from his face. Carissa felt the bottom drop out of her stomach.

"Isn't anybody going to *do* anything?" a girl behind her asked.

"Would you want Maxie to turn on you?" a boy nearby answered.

Were they going to let Maxie pound poor Ziggy to a pulp? Not if *she* could help it! Carissa decided.

She was in the middle of the scene before she realized what she was doing.

"Maxie!"

"What?" He swung around, still holding Ziggy by both arms. Ziggy's arms hung limply at his sides. Carissa could see his bony wrists protruding from beneath his shirtsleeves.

"Put him *down*."

"You got a girl fighting for you now, Zig. I'm getting scared," Maxie growled.

"Grow up, Maxie." Carissa could hardly believe the words she heard from her own mouth. "Pick on someone your own size."

"Someone my own size wouldn't be dumb enough to get me suspended from the wrestling team. I wanted to wrestle tonight."

"You were dumb enough to break the rules on your own, Maxie. Don't blame Ziggy for your mistakes."

A collective gasp filled the hall.

Maxie stared hard at Carissa. "Ain't you Carissa Stevens? The smart one?" He carried on his conversation as though Ziggy weren't suspended between them.

"Well, I—"

"Didn't you tutor me in math a couple years ago?"

"Yes." He'd been a willing pupil, Carissa remembered. In spite of his rough manner, she'd liked him.

"So what're you getting into this for?" Maxie looked puzzled.

"Because I don't want Ziggy pulverized *and* I don't want you in any more trouble. Just sit out the match tonight, Max. If you hurt Ziggy, you'll be put off the team—for good." She wished desperately that Maxie would put Ziggy down. Her mouth was dry, and her legs were beginning to turn to rubber.

She sighed in relief when Maxie finally opened his fists and Ziggy pulled away, rubbing his sore arms. Maxie glared and shook a fist at him. "Don't you go messin' in my stuff anymore, Zig. I'm only lettin' you go 'cause she asked me to. I might not listen to reason next time."

With that, Maxie swung around and sauntered down the hallway as cool and calm as if nothing had happened.

"Are you all right?" Carissa asked anxiously as the crowd in the hallway began to break up.

"I guess so. As all right as someone can be after having a brush with death." Ziggy grinned faintly. "I thought for sure my face was going to be rearranged that time. Maxie was so surprised when you stepped in that he didn't know what to do."

Carissa smiled. "He wasn't the only one surprised. My legs feel like they're going to give out."

"The least I can do is buy my rescuer a shake. What do you say?" Ziggy straightened his collar. "Anyway, let's get out of here."

"Sure. Where to?"

"Andre's. Is that all right?"

Carissa nodded. "It's my favorite place."

"Good. I hear it's dark. We can sit in the back just in case Maxie changes his mind about murdering me. Good thing he'll be over it by tomorrow." Ziggy pushed his hair out of his eyes. "Being student manager is dangerous. They should offer health insurance with the job."

Carissa laughed out loud. It felt good to stand up and be counted for once. She tucked her hand into the arm Ziggy offered, and they strolled down the hall. Soon they were both laughing at Ziggy's close call. Carissa spied Glen in a doorway staring at her. Still laughing, she turned her head proudly. Let Glen see what he was missing!

By six-thirty that night Carissa was already in her robe and slippers. It had started snowing again when she was out with Zig, and the house felt warm and cozy. Julie had a study date with Tom that night, her parents were out, and Ziggy had long ago gone home to recover from his near-miss with Maxie.

Carissa was glad when the phone rang. The house was so quiet she almost wished her parents were home already. She was a bit depressed. Her aunt Carla had sent an early Valentine—a new pair of gloves and a fanciful "Be Mine, Valentine" card with fat cherubs, bows and arrows, and hearts. It only reminded her that the Valentine Ball was nearing—and her chances of having a date for it seemed more remote than ever.

"Hi, Carissa. Were you studying?"

"Rafe! Hello. I was just about to watch television."

"I didn't realize honors students could do that."

"You do, don't you?"

He chuckled. "Only on Sundays. What's on?"

Carissa gave a long explanation of the old movie she was planning to watch at seven-thirty.

At the end of her breathless narration, Rafe asked, "Would you like company?"

Carissa glanced at her ratty robe and worn slippers. "Sure. Give me a few minutes to make some popcorn and . . . things."

"Be there at seven."

By six forty-five, Carissa had changed into soft jeans and an oversized lavender sweatshirt. She'd considered dressing up but finally decided that in order to fully appreciate Spencer Tracy and Katherine Hepburn, she needed to be comfortable. Somehow she knew that Rafe would agree.

"You're just in time," she greeted him at the door. "The butter is ready to pour on the popcorn." Rafe wore jeans as soft and faded as her own. He smiled but didn't speak as Carissa waved him into the living room.

It surprised her sometimes, how quiet Rafe could be. It wasn't an unfriendly silence, more as if he were too tired to speak unnecessarily. Carissa didn't press him. When Rafe had something to tell her, he would. They settled on the couch.

"I love this movie, don't you?" Carissa turned and was surprised to discover how near Rafe was. Somehow, in the course of the movie, his arm had slipped across the back of the couch and around her shoulders.

Now, instead of answering, Rafe leaned forward and brushed his lips against hers. "Salty," he said.

"Popcorn," she said. A giddy feeling washed over her.

"I'd like some more." But Rafe waved aside the popcorn bowl she offered him and instead kissed her again.

"Nice," he finally whispered.

Carissa was so surprised she couldn't believe it. Then he *did* like her! She kissed him back, thinking how very nice it was being wrapped in Rafe's strong arms. She had the feeling their kiss would have gone on if her parents hadn't chosen that moment to return from their meeting at the college. Hurriedly, Rafe took his arms from around her and stood up. He greeted her parents politely and then excused himself.

"I guess I'd better be going now, Carissa. Still have some homework to do. Thanks for the popcorn and the movie," he said as he shrugged into his jacket. At the end of the walk he turned and glanced back as she stood in the doorway. With a faint smile, he raised his right hand to his forehead and saluted. Then he was gone.

Chapter Seven

Seven days and counting to the Valentine Masquerade. And still no date. Carissa stared forlornly out the window. Even the jarring ring of the telephone didn't make her move. Finally, after the fourth ring, she picked up the receiver.

"Hel—"

"Carissa, you've *got* to help me!"

"Hello, Jules. What's the crisis this time?"

"My dress didn't come!"

"What dress?"

"For the Valentine Ball. The one I special-ordered from Dresses Unlimited."

"But that was supposed to be here last week. I heard the saleslady tell you." Julie had found what she considered the perfect dress but had to order it a size smaller than the one in the store. The manager had assured her it would arrive in time.

"And last week she called to say it would be in today. But just now she called again. They made a mistake—it was out of stock! Can you believe it! Only a week until the dance and I don't have a dress!"

"Calm down, Jules. It's Saturday. We can find you another dress."

"They'll all be picked over," Julie wailed. "The only things left will be old enough for my mother to wear."

"I doubt it. Come on over, I'll get dressed. We've got all day to find you a dress."

"And we'll get one for you at the same time," Julie offered, already more cheerful. "Something to set off your gorgeous blond hair."

"And where should I wear it?" Carissa inquired caustically. "To the shower? Or to bed?"

"You mean he hasn't asked you *yet*?" Julie gasped. "What's wrong with Rafe Kelton anyway?"

"Probably nothing. Just because Rafe and I have been working together doesn't mean I can expect him to ask me for a date to the dance." Carissa didn't believe her own words, but she struggled to make them convincing to Julie. "I went steady with Glen for almost a year and a half, and he isn't taking me."

"Because Glen is a first-class jerk," Julie explained with exaggerated patience. "I've told you a million times. Rafe Kelton, well, he has . . . possibilities."

Possibilities. She'd thought so, too, Carissa mused, but apparently she'd been wrong. If Rafe were going to ask her to the dance, surely he would have done it by now. *Especially after our romantic evening at my house . . .*

"Well," Julie concluded, "you'll just have to be prepared. If you haven't looked for a dress, you won't know where to buy one when he does ask you."

I wish I were that sure, Carissa thought. The closer the dance got, the more she wanted to go. When Glen had broken up with her, saying he wanted to date others, she'd thought she'd never care about parties again. But now, with February fourteenth only a week away . . . *Oh Glen! Why did you do this to me?* If they were still together, she'd have a date, instead of all this anxiety.

"Cheer up," Julie consoled her. "Lots of guys haven't made dates yet. They don't have the sense to know how important it is to give the girl a little notice. They think they can

84

give someone a week's notice and presto! The girl will have a dress ready. I just know he'll ask you. In the meantime, you have to be prepared. Have a dress all picked out. I'll pick you up at eleven, and we'll go to the mall."

Julie detailed her plans for the day, and Carissa let her ramble. Julie wasn't ready to believe that her best friend was going to miss the biggest dance ever at Ridgewood High.

Carissa bit her lip. She'd worked at being vivacious and bubbly and thought things had changed. She was more popular than ever at school, and Rafe Kelton, an absolute dream, had actually kissed her! Wasn't she smart enough to snag a date for the Valentine Masquerade?

Head smart and heart smart weren't the same thing, Carissa decided with a sigh. If she'd been smart, she would have stayed as far away from the Valentine committee as she could. That way, it wouldn't have hurt quite so much to stay home.

Then she wouldn't have known about the glittery mirrored balls that would hang from the ceiling of the gymnasium or the red and silver archway in which each couple would be photographed for the souvenir programs. And she wouldn't know that Rafe Kelton had designed the dance floor so that the chaperone's table was on one side of the floor and the gazebo—or the kissing booth, as Rafe jokingly called it—was on the far side. . . .

"So I'll see you then," Julie concluded. "Be ready for a marathon shopping spree!"

Carissa hung up the phone in reflective silence. Everything Rafe did seemed to have a purpose. He never wasted time or energy on things he didn't want to do. Why would he work so hard on a party that *he* wasn't planning to attend?

Or *was* he? Suddenly Carissa felt as though she'd been punched in the stomach. Rafe had never said that he *wasn't* going to the dance. Maybe he was. He and Ziggy were close friends. Ziggy's girlfriend attended another school. What if Rafe had a girlfriend there, too? What if he had a dozen girls in a dozen different places?

Carissa remembered the woman in the big silver car. "Fool," she muttered to herself. She'd overlooked all the obvious signs. Rafe wouldn't work so hard and then stay at home. He'd be there with his mystery girlfriend.

Carissa slumped backward and leaned her head against the wall. She hadn't felt this low since she'd broken up with Glen. What a fool she'd been. No wonder Rafe hadn't discussed his plans for the dance. She was the same tall, smart, *dull* Carissa after all.

Sighing, Carissa began to dress. There was no time to worry anyway. Julie would be there any second.

"What do you think? Too much?" Julie whirled in front of the three-way mirror in Antonio's Boutique.

"You look like you belong on a banana boat."

"What's that supposed to mean?"

"It's the ruffles, Julie. You should have a plate of fruit on your head and platform shoes and castanets in your hands. Haven't you see that guy on TV who—"

"I take it you don't think it's 'right' for me?"

"Sorry, Jules." Carissa slumped onto the nearest chair. "I'm exhausted. Just pick out a dress. Your skin is going to start to peel if you pull another dress over that body."

"But I haven't found the—"

"Perfect dress. Julie, have you considered the fact that it might not exist?"

"Oh, it exists, all right. And I'd better not see some other girl wearing it Saturday night.

Why if Tom's ex-girlfriend shows up in something prettier than—Carissa, there it is!"

"Where?" Carissa didn't even bother to look around. "Just have it delivered to your house so we can go home."

"Not for me, silly! For you! Look at the dress on that mannequin."

To humor Julie, Carissa twisted herself around and gazed after Julie's pointing finger. She blinked and blinked again. Julie was right. Hanging outside the dressing room *was* the perfect dress.

"You've got to try it on, Carissa. Right now. I'll get a saleslady to take it down." Julie began tugging at the huge ruffled bow on her shoulder.

"Whoa! We're looking for a dress for you, Jules, not me."

"But just look at it! You'd be sensational in it!"

Carissa stared at the dress. It was no doubt left over from the Christmas holidays. When else would anyone need a red sequined gown? Except, of course, for a Valentine's Day dance. The mannequin didn't do the dress justice. The neckline was softly rounded, the sleeves long and the lines simple. With sequin-covered fabric around the neckline and cuffs there was no place for nips or tucks or frilly frou-frous. It was elegant and attractive and simple. Julie was right. It was the perfect dress for Carissa.

"Could you get that dress down for me?"- Julie was asking the salesclerk. "The red one with the sequins."

"I'm not sure it would fit you, my dear," the woman said, appraising Julie through the half-glasses hooked to a chain around her neck. "It takes a very tall girl to wear that sort of dress. I'm sure that's why it didn't sell during the holidays. Dozens of women fell in love with it, but none did it justice."

"It's not for me," Julie assured her. "It's for my friend. Stand up, Carissa. Show her how tall you are."

Unwillingly, Carissa unfolded from her chair. The salesclerk's eyes widened with delight.

"You know, you might have just the figure for it. One minute. I'll get a stepladder and take it down."

"Jules," Carissa hissed. "What do you think you're doing?"

"Finding you a dress. Shhh. Here she comes."

The woman bustled over, the dress under her arm. "I'd love to see someone buy this dress. We've marked it down several times, and it still hasn't sold. I'm so fond of it, too." She held it up to Carissa's shoulders. "It looks spectacular with your blond hair."

"So it's cheap?" Julie asked.

"My, yes. Less than half the original price. Whoever gets this dress gets a real bargain."

Julie did a little dance. "Try it on, Carissa. Try it on."

"But I don't need—"

"You never know. And it's a bargain!"

To appease Julie, who would nag at her until she gave in anyway, Carissa took the garment into a dressing room. It was heavy from all the sequins. She draped it across a chair while she slipped out of her jeans and sweatshirt. Methodically she opened the zipper and lifted the dress over her head. It slithered down over her body with a metallic hiss. Keeping her eyes closed, Carissa felt for the zipper and secured it up the back.

Slowly she opened her eyes, and a gasp escaped her. Carissa Stevens was gone. There was someone new and incredibly beautiful in her place.

"Come out and show us," Julie yelped through the dressing-room door. "I want to see what it looks like."

Carissa straightened her shoulders. The neckline dipped modestly to her collarbone. There was no need for jewelry of any kind with a dress like this one. The sleeves ended in a long point below her wrist. The straight, slim skirt glided over her hips as though the dress were made for her. Even the length was perfect. The side opened in a discreet slit partway up her calf. Carissa took a deep breath and opened the door.

Both Julie and the salesclerk were silent. Carissa glanced doubtfully in the mirror. Wasn't it as beautiful as she thought? Why didn't they say anything?

Julie spoke first. "It is absolutely the most incredible dress I have ever seen."

The saleslady cleared her throat. "I knew that dress was made for someone. Obviously it was you. You look lovely, my dear."

"Is it too old-looking?" Carissa frowned. "My parents don't like me to dress too old."

"Well, I've sold several similar dresses to girls at the college." The woman shook her head. "And none have looked as lovely as you."

Julie wore a delighted grin. "It's for a Valentine party at school."

"Perfect!" The woman smiled. "You'll look

like a Valentine yourself. The prettiest one there."

Carissa clawed at the zipper at the back of the dress. "Help me get this off. Now, please."

Confused, the woman hurried to help her. "I didn't offend you, did I? You'll be very lovely. . . ."

"No, you didn't. But I should never have tried it on. I don't need the dress. It was a waste of your time. Please help me unzip it."

As soon as she heard the zipper slide, Carissa rushed into the dressing room. She should never have tried it on. She wasn't going to the dance. What good was the perfect dress when there was no perfect boy to go with it? What did it matter if, for a few moments, she'd felt like a princess? It only made things worse. Much worse.

"Come on, Carissa, don't be like this." Julie peeked her head in the dressing-room door just as Carissa's head poked through the neck of her sweatshirt.

"It was a big mistake to try it on, that's all. We'd better hurry up and find you a dress. I have to be home soon."

Julie gave her a defeated look. "All right. But don't forget about the dress. If—"

"Don't, Julie. Please."

Silently Julie returned to her dressing room. When she emerged again in jeans and a denim jacket, her expression was grim. "If you need to go home, I can keep shopping without you."

"Oh, Jules, I didn't mean to snap like that. It's just . . ."

"I know." Julie's wide blue eyes were teary. "I just can't understand it. You're far and away the prettiest girl I know. You should have had a dozen invitations."

Carissa smiled. "Thanks, friend. Nice try."

"Seriously, I've been thinking. The only thing I can come up with is that you scare guys off. You're tall, you're beautiful, you're super-smart, you're serious . . ."

"I *do* sound pretty scary," Carissa admitted.

"To a teenage boy, at least," Julie agreed. "Glen was just too dumb to know what a good thing he had."

"Don't go running him down again."

"You aren't still sticking up for the creep, are you?"

Carissa glanced down at the floor. There was no use going into it.

"As for Rafe Kelton, I'll never get it." Julie scuffed at the carpet with her shoe. "He's so much like you that if Ken and Barbie ever retired, you and Rafe would be next in line for the job."

"Come off it." Carissa grinned. She couldn't stay glum around Julie and her bizarre comments.

"Think about it. You're tall and blond. He's tall and dark. And he's just as smart as you." Julie looked sly. "I peeked at the honor roll listing on our advisor's desk. He's there, too. *Plus*"—Julie punctuated her remarks with waving hands—"you both act about five years older than you are. You're both so . . . responsible. . . ."

"You don't say it like it's a compliment," Carissa pointed out.

Julie shrugged. "Rafe doesn't fool around like the guys at school. Maybe the rumors *are* true, and he does have an older—" Julie's jaw snapped shut suddenly.

"Older what?"

"Never mind."

"Older girlfriend? Is that what you were going to say? I've thought of that."

"It's just a goofy rumor, that's all. Everybody's seen him getting into that car after school. But that lady could be his sister."

"Would you run home just because your brother was waiting for you?"

94

"No, but . . ."

Carissa sighed.

"Come on, Carissa," Julie pleaded. Then she grinned. "You know what a nerd my brother is."

Carissa had to smile. Anyway, what Rafe Kelton did after school—and who he did it with—was none of her business. He'd shown her that very clearly. He hadn't asked her to the Valentine Masquerade. How much more clear could a message be?

Chapter Eight

"Can you stay to work on decorations to-night?" Mr. Reinhardt asked Rafe that Monday. "I thought if we got the poly backdrop up, tomorrow we could drape the streamers."

Carissa watched from the corner of her eye as Rafe glanced at his watch.

"I suppose so. But I'll have to make a tele-phone call first."

"Fine. Go ahead. Meanwhile, I'll get these guys started. If we work fast, maybe we can get up the wire for the streamers, too."

Mr. Reinhardt's request had gotten in the way of Rafe's plans, Carissa deduced. The woman in the silver car, probably. She turned back to the decoration she was constructing. What did it matter to her? And why were her hands shaking?

"Only five nights until the big one!" Ziggy's voice broke into her reverie. "Hi, Carissa, can I help?"

"Sure, Zig. Have a stapler." She pushed a pile of crepe paper and styrofoam toward him. "Are you ready for the dance?"

"You bet." Ziggy hesitated. "At least I think I am. I'm not a formal sort of dude. I hope I don't blow it."

Carissa gave him an encouraging smile and laid her hand over his. "You'll be a dream date, Zig. I know it."

He gave her a grateful glance. "Thanks. I needed that."

As she worked, Carissa's mind went back to her first meeting with Ziggy. She remembered her nervousness and how her only defense had been to find someone even more anxious than she. She'd come a long way since that first meeting. Julie had been right. It *had* been good for her to serve on this committee—even if she didn't have a date for the dance. She'd learned a lot in the past few weeks. A date now would only be frosting on the cake—the real bonus was what she'd learned about herself.

Glen wandered into the room. His arm looked bare without Tina attached to it. He even looked a little lost and ill at ease.

Carissa leaned back in her chair and studied him. She hadn't thought about Glen in a long time—not really *thought* about him. Rafe was responsible for that. He'd shown her that even without Glen, there were some pretty wonderful people to be her friends.

She was special. Rafe had made her feel it for the first time ever.

Oh Rafe! Why don't you ask me out! But Rafe seemed completely unaware of her feelings.

Impulsively, Carissa turned to Ziggy. "Zig, you know Rafe pretty well, don't you?"

"As well as anyone does, I guess."

"Why doesn't he hang around after school? He looks like such an athlete that I thought maybe he'd go out for sports or . . ."

Ziggy squirmed a bit in his chair. Did he look uncomfortable, Carissa wondered, or was it her imagination?

"I think he has . . . commitments."

"Commitments?"

"You know. Things he has to do." Ziggy stapled the last bit of crepe paper into place. "There. That does it. Now what?"

"Zig!" Mr. Reinhardt yelled, as if on cue. "Come here and help me hold this up!"

"Excuse me." Ziggy quickly rose from his chair.

"Well, I certainly didn't learn anything from him," Carissa muttered. She gathered up the things she was working on.

"Going home?" Glen was suddenly standing near her table.

"Pretty soon. Have you seen Julie?"

"She and Tom were sort of having a—conversation out by the lockers," he answered with a wicked grin.

"Oh." She wasn't in the mood to hear about anyone else's love life—not Julie's or Glen's. Carissa dumped her materials into a large box. "I think I'll work on these at home." She picked up the box and sailed by Glen. His face registered surprise.

Rafe had returned to the room and was standing at the top of a ladder. He turned toward Carissa just as she was about to leave the room. His dark eyes stared down at her.

His expression made her mouth go dry. It was as though he'd said I'm sorry without ever speaking a word.

Sorry? For what, she wondered. Probably for her new dream—the one that would never come true. The dream of Rafe and Carissa.

It was after eight o'clock when the doorbell rang. Carissa shoved her feet into her slippers and shuffled to the door. Her parents were downstairs in the family room and probably hadn't even heard the bell. It was snowing lightly again, and the figure waiting outside was dusted with white powder.

She flicked on the porch light and opened the door.

"Glen! What are you doing here?" She was suddenly extremely conscious of her tattered shirt and paint-spattered jeans.

"Well, can I come in or do I have to talk to you from the front porch?"

"I'm sorry." Carissa stepped aside and waved him into the foyer.

"Thanks." He stomped his feet on the rug and shook his shoulders like a big wet puppy.

"Here, I'll take your coat," Carissa offered.

As Carissa held out her hands, Glen shrugged his jacket away from his shoulders. She didn't mean to, but for just the briefest moment, while Glen turned to make one more swipe at the rug with his shoes, she buried her nose in the collar of his coat.

The sensation was like a physical blow. The familiar scent of his after-shave was overwhelming. She suddenly remembered how it was, going steady with him. *Oh, Glen!*

Quickly she threw the coat over the banister railing, not taking time to hang it in the closet. She didn't want it there, leaving its familiar scent to remind her later of what she'd lost. Composing herself, she followed Glen into the living room.

"Working on the centerpieces, I see." He kicked at the big box on the floor.

"It seemed like an easy thing to do at home."

He dropped onto the couch with familiarity. He seemed perfectly comfortable, as if he'd never been gone. When he looked up, his blue eyes were clear and thoughtful. He stared at Carissa as if he'd never really seen her before.

Carissa sat on the chair across from him and folded her hands in her lap. Finally he spoke.

"You've surprised me, Carissa."

"Oh?" She tilted her head to one side. "How?"

He shifted his long legs and threw his arm across the back of the couch. Carissa could remember when she was welcome in the curve of his arm.

"I never thought you'd actually do it—stay on the steering committee for the Valentine's party."

"We volunteered at the same time, if you remember."

"Yeah, but I thought you were just staying on to . . ." He had the grace to look embarrassed. "To show me a thing or two. I figured you'd drop out after a few meetings."

"You didn't think I could do it on my own?"

He looked vaguely troubled. "I didn't think you would, that's all."

"Because I'm shy?"

"I suppose." He paused. "But you don't seem so shy anymore."

For some reason this conversation—the one that she had thought would make her happy—was making her angry.

"Maybe I was never as shy as you thought I was. Maybe you just never made the effort to really get to know me."

"Then that was my mistake."

Was Glen looking regretful? Carissa wished Julie were here to see it.

"I realize now that you don't like 'shy' girls," Carissa pointed out. "You like outgoing girls like Tina Walters."

"I thought I did." Glen suddenly didn't look so comfortable on the couch.

"*Thought* you did? Past tense?"

"Don't give me an English lesson, Carissa." Glen frowned in that way he had when she'd irritated him. "Maybe I didn't realize what I wanted until recently."

"And what *do* you want?" Where was she getting this courage? From the pent-up fury she'd stored since Glen had left her?

"Someone who's a little more . . . stable. Someone who doesn't flit around from person to person." He shifted on the couch. "You know, I really thought I wanted a girl who was outgoing and liked parties and was always on the go, but I was wrong, Carissa. I didn't know a good thing when I had it. When I had you."

There they were, the words she'd longed to hear. Glen leaned forward on the couch, his elbows resting on his knees, his hands folded together.

"I want you back, Carissa. And I'd like to take you to the Valentine Masquerade."

She stared at him for a long time. There was no use speaking. Her pounding heart would have drowned out her words. Glen's eyes pleaded with hers. Finally Carissa found her voice.

"She dumped you, huh?"

Where was a camera when you needed one? The dumbfounded expression on Glen's face was worth millions.

"What did you say?"

"Tina dumped you. For another guy," Carissa

said matter-of-factly. "And right before the Valentine Masquerade. That wasn't very nice of her."

"How did you know. . . ."

"I didn't know," she assured him coolly. "I guessed. Why else would you be over here tonight?"

"I told you, Carissa . . ." Glen's voice faded away as he blushed hotly.

"Because you discovered that a quiet girl wasn't such a bad thing? Because she might not leave you for another guy?"

"I know you're still mad, but be reasonable."

"Reasonable? About what?" She'd never felt so many conflicting emotions before. She was very angry and hurt and . . . longing to go to the dance.

"So I learned the hard way that Tina wasn't such a good idea! I also learned that I didn't appreciate you enough."

"Because I never would have dumped you right before a big party, right?"

Glen dipped his head. "I know that now. I'm really sorry, Carissa."

Why was it so difficult staying mad at him! Carissa closed her eyes. What had happened to her usual common sense?

"At least go to the Valentine Masquerade

with me, Carissa. For old time's sake." He spread his hands wide, his voice grew soft. "We had some good times together. We could have even more."

She stood up and paced across the room. "I don't know, Glen. I don't know anything. You've caught me totally by surprise. I need to think."

Sensing a partial victory, Glen jumped up. "Okay. Think. But let me know soon." He took her hand. "Say yes?"

She pulled away and hurried across the room. With one hand she grabbed Glen's coat, and with the other she jerked open the door. "I'll call you."

"Tonight?"

"Maybe. I don't know." Why didn't he leave? Why did he stand there looking as though he wanted to kiss her?

Finally he raised a finger to her lips. "I'll be waiting." Then, flipping his coat over his head and sliding his arms into the sleeves, he disappeared into the night.

"Answer, Jules! You've got to answer!"

Carissa let Julie's phone ring a dozen times more, then hung up, staring at the phone in disgust. Just when she needed to talk to Julie, she wasn't home. Fine best friend she was.

Carissa's parents were still engrossed in an old musical comedy on television in the family room. They didn't even know what had just happened upstairs.

Carissa stared at the phone, willing it to ring. She needed to talk to someone—she needed Julie's support.

Maybe something was wrong with it. She couldn't remember hearing it ring all evening, and since she couldn't reach Julie . . . no good, she admonished herself. The phone was in perfect working order. It was her love life that was messed up.

Rafe Kelton, why don't you ever call me?

Carissa dropped her head into her cupped hands. What was so wrong with her that Rafe didn't call? They'd had so much fun together— eating at Andre's, going to the gallery, planning for the Valentine dance, getting to know each other. Oh, why didn't he call with an invitation to the dance? One call from Rafe would solve everything.

"What's wrong, honey?" Mrs. Stevens strolled into the living room and eyed her daughter curiously. "Do you have a headache?"

Heartache was more like it. Carissa shook her head. "Yes. No. I'm not sure."

Her mother's eyebrows arched. "Want to explain that?"

"Glen was just here," Carissa said with a sigh.

"Glen Matlock?" Even the normally imperturbable Mrs. Stevens looked surprised. "But I thought . . ."

"So did I. But it seems his girlfriend found someone new, and he wants me back."

"I see."

Her mother's expression was calm. Carissa knew immediately that she wouldn't get any help there. Mrs. Stevens prided herself on letting Carissa make her own decisions. Carissa appreciated it—most of the time.

"Should I go, Mom?"

"Do you want to?"

"I want to go to the dance. I've worked really hard to make it special. The band is going to be great—everyone says so. . . ." Her voice trailed away.

"Then why are you hesitating?"

"Because . . . you see . . . I'm not sure. . . ."

Mrs. Stevens briefly put her arm around Carissa's shoulders. "Sounds to me like you have some more thinking to do, Carissa. Just remember. Be true to yourself. Do what's best for you."

Carissa nodded morosely as her mother walked out of the room. Wasn't that just like a mother? Making her act like a grown-up when, for once, she longed to be a child—who was told what to do.

Grown-up, mature, adult. Those were concepts much nicer to think about than to actually become, Carissa decided. She'd always prided herself on being mature. That was part of what attracted her to Rafe—his responsible, adult manner. And the lack of it was one of the things she'd liked least about Glen.

But did it really matter if your date was mature or childish when it was only for one evening? The most important evening of the year?

With thoughts of beautiful red streamers and glittery Mylar balloons whirling in her head, Carissa picked up the telephone.

Chapter Nine

"Hello." On the other end of the line, Glen's voice was so familiar and yet so foreign. How could a few weeks turn someone you thought you loved into a stranger?

"It's me, Carissa," she answered.

"Hi." His voice was warm, eager and a little nervous. "Have you decided?"

"Yes."

"Well?"

She could picture the mirrored ball spinning and the red and silver streamers fluttering as the Grass Roots played.

"I can't go with you, Glen."

The silence at the other end of the line seemed to go on forever. When he finally spoke, his voice was muted and hurt. "If *that's* the way you feel about it, Carissa. I never thought you'd be the type to . . ."

"To what, Glen?"

"To play games."

"This isn't a game. And I'm not trying to hurt you or get revenge, no matter what you think. But I do have some pride, Glen." His silence somehow encouraged her to continue.

"For a long time I really thought that I loved you." The ache in her throat was very real. "I learned that it wasn't as serious an emotion as all that, but I still won't use you. I'm just not that kind of a person."

"Use me?" His voice was strangled.

Images of Rafe flooded her mind. "Yes, use you—to get places and to do things that I'd like to do, even though I don't have any feelings left for you. I have to go now, Glen." She paused. "And thanks anyway."

Carefully Carissa placed the receiver into its cradle. A gentle smile lit her features.

"Who was on the phone, honey?" Mrs. Stevens returned from the kitchen with a huge bowl of popcorn.

"Glen."

"And what did you decide?"

Carissa gave a small sigh. "I decided that if I couldn't be at this party with a boy I really cared about, I wouldn't go at all."

Her mother smiled. "And would that be Rafe Kelton?"

"How did you know?"

"I haven't been your mother for sixteen years for nothing." She put her free arm around Carissa's shoulders. "Come downstairs and join your dad and me. There's a *very* romantic movie on television. I think you're just the type to appreciate it."

Carissa Stevens, you are awesome. Really! I am so *proud* of you!" Julie's expression was rapt. "You gave Glen Matlock exactly what he deserved—a dose of his own rejection." She rubbed her hands together gleefully. "The jerk."

"I didn't do it to hurt Glen," Carissa chided. "What's the point? It just didn't seem all that important to go anymore." She gave a shrug that was far more casual than she felt. "I'm a big girl. I don't have to go to every party."

"Unless, of course, Rafe Kelton goes, too." Julie's voice was sly and knowing.

"Is Rafe going to the dance?" Carissa wished her heart would stop pounding so wildly.

"I don't know, but I have a hunch that if he asked you, you'd be very interested."

Carissa's reserve crumbled. "Oh, Jules, I really thought I wanted to get Glen back, to be on his arm for the Valentine Masquerade. Last night I got my chance, and I gave it up. Maybe I'm losing my mind."

"Not likely. Just getting a grip on it, I'd say. You were goofy over Glen, and he was never all that crazy about you. You deserve a guy who really appreciates you. Like Rafe."

"Why do you say that?"

"Because you and Rafe are a lot alike. You're both creative and intense." Julie waggled her eyebrows. "You and Rafe would be dynamite together."

"If we ever get together."

"Yeah." Julie frowned. "And even I don't know how to make that happen only three days before a dance."

Two days and counting. The decorations were nearly complete. Carissa was so busy she almost managed to keep Rafe at the back of her mind—almost.

But when she stood in the middle of the gym, which had been turned into a fairyland, and gazed at the miles of streamers, the dazzling mirrored balls that hung from the ceiling, and the huge and fanciful masks gazing from silver pillars, her insides twisted into knots.

Rafe had been around very little the past two days. It was as though he knew he was the cause of her unhappiness and didn't want to be there to view her misery.

It was Friday afternoon after her last class that he caught her in the hallway.

"Carissa, we've got to talk." His fingers closed around her elbow with a surprising firmness.

"Huh? Well, okay. I just have to drop some napkins off in the gym, and I'm done for the day." Her heart was thudding like a war drum, but she managed to act cool.

"Can you go to Andre's?"

"I suppose so."

He stood impatiently at the doorway while she delivered the red and silver napkins to the punch table. She had a hard time keeping up with him as he led the way to Andre's.

The last booth was open. Usually only the most serious couples—those with really private things to say—took that booth. Rafe steered her toward it without hesitation.

Once they were settled, with two untouched dishes of ice cream between them, Rafe leaned his elbows on the table.

"Is something wrong?" Carissa asked. "You aren't sick or anything, are you?"

He glanced up with a shadow of a grin. "No, but that would be a better excuse than the one I've got."

She felt as though she'd missed something. What was he talking about? "Excuse? For what?"

"For not asking you to the Valentine Masquerade."

If Andre's ceiling had fallen in at that moment, Carissa would not have noticed.

"I . . . I don't understand."

Rafe's dark eyes were sad. "I wanted to ask you a long time ago but I didn't want to rush things too much. Then my situation changed, and I couldn't."

"Couldn't ask me?"

"It had nothing to do with you, Carissa. Vicky's plans changed."

"Vicky?" A jealous twinge shot through her. She didn't like the sound of this—not one bit.

Rafe grinned apologetically. "Vicky Kelton. My mom."

"You call your mother Vicky?"

"That's her name."

"Whatever happened to *Mom* or *Mother*?" Carissa asked curiously. "And what plans?"

"I can see that I'd better start at the very beginning." Rafe laughed. "Otherwise none of this is going to make sense."

"I think you're right." Carissa folded her hands on the table. She was most definitely ready to listen.

Rafe's expression was serious as he began. "Well, Mom likes me to call her by her name since she's so young and all. Anyway, Vicky— Mom—married my dad when she was seventeen and my dad was twenty-one."

"That sounds young," Carissa murmured, wondering where all this was leading.

"Too young. Maybe that's why they didn't stay together. They divorced when I was three."

"I'm sorry."

He tilted his head. "It's okay. Vicky worked, and I stayed with my grandmother during the day until I was old enough to go to school. We lived in New Mexico then." He grinned suddenly. "You know, after we moved here, the first time I saw snow I nearly went berserk."

She returned his smile. Then his eyes grew serious again.

"Vicky remarried when I was ten. That's

when she had her 'second' family. I have two little brothers, five and four, and a baby sister who just turned two."

"Really?" Carissa grinned. "I love little kids. I wish I'd known."

Rafe's expression darkened, but he didn't speak until Carissa touched his arm with her fingertip. "Go on."

"Sorry." Rafe pulled himself back to the present. "Anyway, my stepdad was a great guy. . . ."

"Was?"

"Bill was killed in a car accident two years ago, just before my sister was born."

"Oh, Rafe!" No wonder he seemed to bear the worries of the world on his shoulders. He'd had to get used to a new father, only to lose him as well.

He shrugged. "It's okay. We're doing all right. Bill left us a lot of insurance money. That's why Vicky—Mom—decided to go back to school."

"Your mother is in college?"

"Yeah." He smiled proudly. "She's almost a junior. She's moving fast. She wants to be a social worker so she can help people who've had troubles like hers." Rafe nodded thoughtfully. "My mom is really sharp. She's going to be great."

Carissa suddenly realized why her father had recognized the Kelton name—he'd no doubt had Rafe's mother in a class.

Rafe chuckled. "Vicky's beautiful, too. The guys tease me when she picks me up after school. They think I've got a college girl on the string." He laughed out loud. "Imagine what they'd think if they knew it was my mother!"

The woman in the big silver car! Things were suddenly falling into place.

"Yeah, imagine that." Carissa laughed weakly. She hoped Rafe couldn't see her blushing. She'd also thought there was an older woman in Rafe's life.

"But why does she want you home so quickly? I've seen how you hurry out the door after class."

"Vicky has a language lab in the afternoon. I have to get home to baby-sit."

"To baby-sit?"

Rafe grinned sheepishly. "Sounds wimpy, I know. But my mother likes the idea of the little guys having family around rather than baby-sitters and . . ." He paused for a moment. "I think about how it was for me when I was growing up. I was lonely a lot of the time. My grandmother wasn't good at keep-

117

ing up with a little guy like me, so she'd just have me sit in front of the television until my mother came home."

When he looked at her, Carissa felt that she might melt with tenderness. "I guess I wanted these three to have it better than I did. And Vicky feels good knowing I'm with the kids. She really depends on me."

No wonder he acts so grown-up. He's had to be.

"Why didn't you say anything, Rafe?" Carissa asked gently. "It would have been so much easier to understand you if I'd known."

"You might have understood. But try to tell the guys on a football team that you can't play because you've promised your mother you'll baby-sit."

"B-but . . ." She stammered to a halt. It was all so unexpected.

"Ziggy knows. He's been great. He also knows I prefer not to have my after-school activities publicized." Rafe shrugged. "Now you know my entire, sordid past."

"It's not sordid," Carissa declared. "It's wonderful. Your brothers and sister are very lucky."

"Yeah? Maybe so, but it sure has messed up my social life. Every time I stay after school

I have to call and make baby-sitting arrangements." He looked at her fondly. "You've been hard on my credibility as a reliable baby-sitter."

Carissa couldn't stop staring at him. Rafe Kelton, was so handsome, so mature, so tender! It was like finding a gold mine in her backyard, Carissa thought.

Much to her surprise, Rafe wrapped his fingers gently around her own. "And now I get to the hard part."

"What's that?"

"Why I didn't ask you to the Valentine Masquerade."

Her contented feeling vanished. "Oh."

"I really meant to, until Vicky's field trip came up."

"Field trip?"

"Yeah. Her class was going to Chicago for a week to work with social workers at a crisis center. People who could teach them a lot."

"And?"

"And they were supposed to leave today at four o'clock."

"I see."

Rafe rubbed her hands gently, massaging the tightness away. "Vicky's not very good at leaving the kids. Especially since Bill . . ." His voice trailed away, and Carissa could tell that he was remembering something very sad. Then he glanced up at her. "Anyway, she made me promise I'd be home for the kids every minute. They would be in day-care while I was in school and then I would take them home with me."

Rafe looked apologetic. "I know it sounds weird, but Vicky is terrified that something might happen to her, too, and the little guys might not have anyone to take care of them."

He shuffled his feet under the table, and his leg brushed against Carissa's. She shivered. "She wouldn't go at all until I promised to be with them." His eyes turned pleading. "You understand, don't you?"

Carissa nodded. There *had* been another girl fouling up her chances for the Valentine Masquerade—a mother and a two-year-old!

Rafe gave a low, wry laugh. "And now it's all fallen through anyway."

"What did you say?" Carissa shook her head in confusion. "What's fallen through?"

"Vicky's field trip. She just called me. They're going the first week of March. Her instructor couldn't get things set up for this weekend." Rafe's hands tightened around her own. "And here I am, with a weekend all to myself and no place to go."

"What about the Valentine's dance?" Carissa asked softly. "Can't you go to that?"

"I don't think so."

"Why not?" Her heart was thudding hard in her chest.

"Because the girl I wanted to go with is already taken."

He looked so disappointed, Carissa ached for him. But she was disappointed, too—not to mention confused. "I thought you said you were going to ask me."

Startled, he glanced up at her. "But you're going with Glen Matlock."

"Who told you that?"

"Ziggy. He overheard Matlock bragging about it in the locker room." Rafe's expression darkened. "Matlock said he was going to 'pick up where he left off.' "

"Oh, he did, did he?" Carissa growled. "Imagine that." Julie was right: Glen *was* a jerk!

"That's what Ziggy heard."

"But Ziggy couldn't hear everything in the locker room."

"He couldn't?"

"No. He couldn't hear me turn down Glen's invitation."

A smile began to spread slowly across Rafe's

121

face. "No, I guess Ziggy couldn't hear that. Any special reason why you did that?"

"Because"—Carissa boldly grasped Rafe's wrists—"I didn't want to go to the party with just anyone. I decided it was better to stay home."

"I see." A crooked, half-naughty, half-daring smile lit Rafe's face. "And do I fit under the heading of 'just anyone?' "

"You'll have to ask me and find out."

Rafe straightened his shoulders and shook a stray lock of hair out of his eyes. He licked his lips nervously and smiled at her again. He looked incredibly appealing.

"Miss Stevens, would you go to the Valentine Masquerade with me tomorrow night?"

"Mr. Kelton, I would love to."

As Rafe's lips descended upon her own, Carissa remembered thinking that the back booth at Andre's was the most wonderful, most romantic place in the entire world.

Chapter Ten

"But I don't have a dress!" Carissa paced across the pale peach carpet of Julie's bedroom. "Or shoes or jewelry. Nothing! How can I go to the dance?" She sank onto Julie's bed. "I'll have to tell him I can't go."

Julie flipped from her back to her stomach and waggled a disapproving finger in the air. "No way. You've come this far, and nothing is going to stop you now. You've got plenty of time to get ready."

"And what am I supposed to wear? The only long dress I have is from last year's prom. It's much too sheer to wear to a winter dance. I even looked in Mom's closet, but her clothes are too old for me."

"Not to worry," Julie commented calmly.

She secured the top on the bottle of nail polish she was using and waved her hands to dry her nails.

"That's easy for you to say," Carissa complained.

"You keep forgetting," Julie reminded her, "that you have a super-duper, one-of-a-kind, incredible best friend. I can help you with a dress."

"How?"

"What about a fabulous red dress with sequined neckline and cuffs?"

"Do you think . . ." Carissa looked hopeful for a moment, then her face fell. "No way that dress is still there—especially on sale. It's too gorgeous."

"True—unless someone fantastic asked the saleslady to hold it for a few days," Julie said slyly. Casually she checked to see if her nails were dry.

"What?"

Julie grinned widely. "I was in Dresses Unlimited yesterday. The dress was still there. The clerk remembered me, and said she'd hold the dress until today 'just in case.' She said there weren't many people that could wear a dress like that one. She said if any other six-foot blonds came into the store, she'd have to show it to them, but . . ."

"She's holding it till *today*?" Carissa grabbed Julie's arm and yanked her off the bed. "What are we waiting for? Let's pick up my dress!"

It was even more beautiful than she'd remembered, Carissa decided.

She allowed Julie and the enthusiastic salesclerk to outfit her in whatever they wanted— silk slip, low-heeled pumps, and gold earrings with a tiny red stone that glittered in the light.

"Look out, Rafe Kelton!" Julie clapped her hands in delight. "He won't know what hit him!"

"Oh, Jules." Carissa grabbed her friend's hands. "I'm so nervous, I think I'm going to—"

"Calm down. Think how far you've come. Remember the red-eyed, weepy person moaning over losing Glen Matlock to Tina Walters? Remember the person who thought she was too shy to find another guy?" Julie spun Carissa toward the three-way mirror in the dressing room. "See that person in the mirror? Any resemblance?"

Not a bit, Carissa decided. The old Carissa never flung her shoulders back and stood so tall. And *never* had the old Carissa looked so pleased with herself. She had come a long way—and she wasn't going back.

"We'd better take this home to show my folks. This is the first time ever that Mom gave approval to a dress without seeing it first."

"That's because she understands our deadline," Julie responded calmly. "Anyway, you're too sensible to do anything foolish."

"I was," Carissa teased. "Let's hope they still think so when they see this dress."

But there was no need to worry. Mr. and Mrs. Stevens were as delighted with the dress as she and Julie were. While Mr. Stevens stared, Carissa's mother shot out of the room. She returned carrying a tiny box.

"What's that, Mom?"

"Something I've been saving for a special occasion." Mrs. Stevens slowly opened the box. Inside was a tiny gold ring with two hearts entwined.

"It's beautiful," Carissa gasped. "Where did you get it?"

"From your dad." A soft glow lit Mrs. Steven's features. "He gave it to me for Valentine's Day the year before we were married."

"Why don't you wear it?" Gently Carissa lifted the ring from its case.

"Too fragile, I guess. It seemed better to put it away and keep it safe."

"Why did you bring it out now?" Carissa turned the ring in her hand. It reflected the soft light of the room.

"Because I'd like you to wear it tomorrow night."

"Mom!"

Mrs. Stevens smiled. "This ring was part of a very romantic time in my life. I'd like you to feel that way, too—and to wear it to the Valentine Masquerade."

"But you never offered it to me when I was dating Glen," Carissa pointed out.

Her mother gave an ingenuous smile. "Was it appropriate then?"

Mother and daughter stared at each other. Then Carissa started to grin. She flung her arms around her mother. "I hope I'm as wise as you when I have a daughter."

Carissa felt she must have aged ten years in the last hour and a half. If Rafe didn't get there soon, he was going find a haggard-looking date with a face etched with worry lines! Carissa glanced in the mirror. No sign of that yet, thank goodness. Her blond hair lay in thick golden waves across her shoulders. Her pale red lips framed even, white teeth. Outwardly she looked cool and calm.

But where was Rafe? It was nearly seven o'clock!

She and Rafe and the rest of the decorating committee had spent most of that morning adding finishing touches to the gym. It was completely unrecognizable now. The bleachers were hidden behind plastic poly walls, and the basketball hoops were covered by silver columns wrapped in foil.

Carissa pressed her hands together nervously. The decorations had exceeded even the committee's expectations. Everything would be beautiful—if Rafe would only arrive. . . .

Though she'd been waiting for it all evening, when the doorbell rang Carissa jumped as though a bullet had gone off near her ear. She could hear her father greeting Rafe at the bottom of the stairs.

"Well, this is it," she told herself. "The first appearance of the butterfly from the cocoon." The new and more confident Carissa Stevens was about to make her grand entrance—if she didn't come apart at the seams first.

As her foot touched the step at the top of

the stairs, she saw Rafe's shoulders stiffen. He glanced up at her, and she gazed down at him. He wore a black tuxedo, a pristine white shirt, and a red cumberbund and bow tie. His black shoes were so highly polished that they gleamed in the hall light. Every strand of hair—even the stubborn bangs that often fell appealingly over his eye—had been tamed. But it wasn't his appearance that gave her the greatest pleasure. It was the look on his face.

His eyes had never looked darker, and they shone with unabashed delight. His eyes said everything she needed to know.

"Hi, Rafe." Carissa willed her legs to hold her steady as she descended the stairs.

"Hello, yourself." His gaze had the intensity of a touch. "You are *beautiful*."

Carissa blushed and glanced at her father. The expression on his face said he completely agreed.

Teasingly Carissa told Rafe. "You aren't so bad yourself."

Rafe gave a playful toss of his shoulders and straightened his tie. "I tried." Then he bent to pick up the florist's box on the chair. "Want to try these on for size?"

Slowly, carefully, savoring each moment,

Carissa opened the box. Inside was a cluster of tiny red roses on a bed of white baby's breath.

Rafe cleared his throat. "I hope you don't mind, but I called Julie about the flowers. I wanted to surprise you, and she suggested something for your hair. Is that all right?"

"All right? It couldn't be more perfect."

As Carissa secured the flowers in her hair, her mother went to the refrigerator and returned with the red rose boutonniere Carissa had purchased for Rafe.

"Red again. You and I will be the perfect Valentine couple," he said, obviously pleased.

She watched him from the corner of her eye. He was so confident, so secure, so mature. All the things she admired in him seemed even more apparent tonight. Rafe Kelton—mystery man, baby-sitter, friend. What a combination—and what a night it was going to be!

"Ready?" Rafe offered his arm with a gallant gesture.

Carissa's mother, looking suspiciously misty eyed, tossed her own white cape across her daughter's shoulders as Carissa wound her arm into Rafe's.

The snow was drifting from the sky in big, puffy flakes.

"I ordered it this way just for you," Rafe teased. "So you could catch the flakes on your tongue and feel them melt. How do you like it?"

"Perfect. And you have your mother's car, I see."

"Nothing but the best." He ushered her to the side of the car and opened the door with a flourish. As Carissa started to slide into the car, Rafe stopped her with a gentle touch.

"I wish this car didn't have bucket seats. I don't want you away from my side this entire evening."

Carissa shivered with anticipation at the magical time that awaited them.

The school was lit from top to bottom when they arrived. Rafe parked near the door and turned off the ignition. Before getting out of the car, however, he put his arm around Carissa's shoulders. His face was so close to hers she could feel the warmth of his breath against her cheek.

"I heard the band warming up earlier. They're good. Really good."

"Mmmmm." It was all she could manage.

"Ziggy is in his glory. He set up and the Grass Roots let him try out their equipment. Plus he did all the lighting. According to him, there are going to be some great effects."

"Good. I'm glad Zig is finally getting his big chance."

"Yeah. It all looks perfect. There's one thing missing, though." His brow furrowed.

"Oh? What? Something important?"

"This." And he leaned forward and kissed her.

If the night had ended at that moment, it would have been enough for Carissa. Rafe smiled.

"Come on. Otherwise I might forget all about the band and those decorations and all our hard work and just take you to Andre's. I'll bet that back booth is empty tonight."

The gymnasium was a moving mass of color. Formals, tuxedos, and flowers were everywhere. Mr. Reinhardt was pacing in front of the doorway muttering to himself.

"Something wrong, sir?" Rafe smiled brightly. Obviously nothing could mar his mood for the rest of the evening.

"The food committee—they failed me. I can't believe it. The punch is here and that's fine, but the buffet table . . ."

"Aren't Glen Matlock and Tina Walters in charge of that?"

Was that a chuckle in Rafe's voice? Carissa couldn't be sure.

"Yes. Talk about miscommunication. Those two had a falling out before they got their committee together. Glen thought Tina was ordering the food trays and Tina thought Glen was going to do it. Then they quit speaking to each other."

Carissa clamped a hand over her mouth to keep from laughing out loud.

"I just sent Glen to the twenty-four-hour store to see if they can make some trays immediately. Tina's in the home ec room dumping tortilla chips and pretzels into bowls. The hot sauce is here somewhere."

Rafe turned to Carissa, his eyebrow cocked comically. "I knew I was on the right committee."

Before Carissa could reply, Julie came barreling toward them, a grinning Tom in tow.

"You two are the most incredibly gorgeous couple here," Julie announced. "Of course, Tom and I aren't so bad ourselves. Are we?" She snuggled into his arm, and the grin on his face grew.

"Tom's not a man of many words," Julie

explained to Rafe—as if it weren't already obvious—"but I'm a woman of *lots* of words. That's why we get along so well. Look! Here comes Ziggy!"

If she hadn't known him so well, Carissa would never have recognized Ziggy. He wore a dark suit, a crisp white shirt, and a cheery red tie. His hair, usually mussed, was cut and groomed to perfection. The smile on his face was radiant.

"Hi, guys! I want you to meet my date. Everyone, this is Penny Vallen."

While Zig went through the introductions, Carissa studied Penny. She was small and delicate, with large brown eyes. Her smile was timid but pleasant, and the looks she gave Ziggy told Carissa that he'd picked exactly the right date.

She glanced again at Rafe. He was so handsome—and he was hers. She felt incredibly lucky.

"Ziggy, why don't you and Penny share a table with the four of us?" Julie asked.

"Sure. Thanks."

"It'll be fun." Julie turned to Carissa and Rafe. "There are some tables for six, right?"

Just as Carissa was about to agree, Rafe said, "Thanks, Julie, but I've reserved a little table for two. You understand," he added with a wink.

"So that's how it is," Julie said delightedly. "Have fun. You can always come and visit."

As Rafe escorted her across the dance floor to a secluded table, Carissa demanded, "But how did you . . ."

"I designed the layout, remember?"

"But you hadn't asked me. . . ."

"That's why I came back earlier. To put a reserved sign on the table. And this." On the table lay a single long-stemmed red rose. Rafe picked it up and put it in her hand.

Carissa wanted to speak, but the words caught in her throat.

His gaze roamed her face. They were oblivious to the noise and movement around them.

"You're a very special girl, Carissa Stevens." Rafe put a finger to her lips. "Before you deny it, let me finish."

His expression grew somber. "I never took part in much at Ridgewood. Mostly because of my family situation, but there were other reasons. The girls I met were into fun—lots of dates and parties and stuff. I'd disappoint them." He smiled. "I'm a pretty serious guy. But between family and school I was getting pretty dull. Then I met you."

Carissa held her breath.

"You're beautiful and intelligent and caring. I still remember how nice you were to Ziggy." His eyes were dark and serious. "I think we care about the same things, Carissa. I hope that's true."

She placed her hands over his. "That's the nicest thing anyone has ever said to me."

"The nicest?" He leaned forward until their lips and noses were almost touching.

"Definitely."

"What if I said I was the luckiest guy at Ridgewood because the most beautiful girl in the room is at my table?"

"That's a close second."

"Or that I never felt like this about anyone before?"

Her mouth went dry.

"Or that I've been waiting to do this ever since we walked into the room?" His lips touched hers.

When she finally pulled away, she said, "That is definitely the nicest thing I've ever heard."

Rafe extended his hand."Want to dance?"

Carissa glanced at him in surprise. "But the band isn't playing yet."

"Does it matter?" He entwined her fingers in his. "I hear romantic music of my own."

The old Carissa would have dissolved in embarrassment. Without hesitating, Carissa stood up.

"I'd love to dance, Rafe."

The mirrored ball spun and glittered in the center of the room. Chatting couples made way for the band members to move toward the stage. But Rafe and Carissa, in their secluded corner, already danced to their own perfect rhythm.